THE CENTAUR'S BRIDE

A STEAMY MYTHOLOGY ROMANCE

TAMSIN LEY

D1713523

A Production of
Twin Leaf
Press

ISBN: 1545108390
ISBN-13: 978-1545108390

*B*lack Stevens pushed the brim of his cowboy hat up off his forehead with the back of a wrist and stepped aside to allow the newborn foal room to stand. Dim florescent bulbs hanging from the barn's rafters fought back the night with tenacious insistence. The delivery had gone smoothly, in spite of the herd's concern that Millie was too old for another pregnancy.

Beside him, Millie's oldest daughter, Su, let out a sigh of relief. "She looks okay?"

"Right as rain," he said, meeting her gaze.

Su quickly looked away. In her human form, Su was even more mousy than her horse form, with nondescript dark hair and sallow skin that matched her mare coat.

She was one of the few herd members subordinate to Black.

Millie, a bay, bumped her gray-haired muzzle against the newborn, encouraging her to stand.

"What're you going to name her?" Black asked.

Millie snorted and rolled an eye, unable to answer in horse form, while Su held out a hand to the filly, sharing her smell. "We'll probably let Lori decide."

Now it was Black's turn to snort and roll his eyes. He hooked his thumbs into the front loops of his jeans rather than ball his hands into fists like he wanted to. Since his grandmother's death, Lori had taken over as Lead Mare and had all but declared martial law over the herd.

"Let me decide what?" Lori's sultry voice filled the barn. Black ducked around the stall corner to find the blonde-haired herd leader approaching, decked in what she called her human bling—lacy black bra peeking above the plunge of her red button-down shirt, tight jeans with bright rivets along the pockets, and a big silver belt buckle shaped like the state of Montana. Her shiny New Helens cowboy boots brought her almost eye-to-eye with Black's six-foot-three frame.

"Hey, soldier." She sauntered past him, keeping her gaze locked with his until he looked away like a good herd member. A lifetime of ingrained respect for rank warred with his urge to buck the new Lead Mare's authority. Stallions protected the herd physically, while mares guided policy, and the lead mare's word was law once she was voted in. Only the strongest herd members might dare to challenge her. His grandmother had demanded respect during her leadership, but she'd also given it in return. Lori was just a bully.

Inside the birthing stall, Lori took a wide stance, hands on her hips. "Well she's a plain-Jane little thing, isn't she? Let's call her Jane, shall we?"

Su kept her chin down and nodded, while Millie turned her head aside submissively.

Black's nostrils flared, but he kept his posture relaxed. "I thought we might name her Ivy because of those lovely stripes wrapping her hocks."

The herd leader flicked her manicured fingers dismissively. "Ivy's for greener pastures. We'll stick with Jane. Come on, ladies. We're heading out." She snaked her belt off and hung it from a peg near the entrance as if staking territory with a flag, then pulled off her boots. She shoved them at Black. "Put these in my locker."

Before he could blink, Lori and Su were naked, Lori's upright breasts and perfectly manicured pubic area a complete opposite to Su's natural sags and bulges. Lori slipped into the darkness outside. Su followed close behind, casting a concerned glance over her shoulder at Millie. The light spilling from the open door caught a flash of Lori's golden palomino coat as she shifted.

Millie nudged her new foal toward the exit.

"You don't need to go. Let Ivy-Jane get her legs and nurse." Black refused to call the baby plain Jane. "She should meet your human form, too." Black put a hand on Millie's bony whither, self-conscious about giving a seasoned mother advice, but his veterinary training wouldn't allow him to remain silent. Not only were there dangers like mountain lions out there, but the first few hours of a foal's life were critical for imprinting, especially for shifter young, who had to acquaint themselves with what amounted to two mothers. The foal wouldn't be capable of shifting for a few years, but she'd have to learn both equine and human communication right away.

The mare's scarred flank flinched at his touch. She turned her head to bump against him with her cheek, telling him she appreciated his concern, but to mind his own.

He sighed and stepped back, listening as the sound of hooves striking packed dirt faded into the night. Stuffing Lori's clothes into a cubby, he looked around for any spectators before he stripped down himself. As a centaur, he'd never be a true part of the herd, and had to guard his secret more diligently than the other shifters, but tonight he had a foal to protect.

Taking a breath, he faced the door and allowed the pressure of the shift to take hold.

*R*enee angled the rented Ford Escape up the dirt hill toward the ranch's gate, air conditioner running full blast against the dry Montana heat. Her best friend, Steph, sat in the passenger seat, scrolling through her phone, already bored with the sagebrush-covered hills and stark rock formations rimming the plateau. Decades-old memories tumbled over Renee as they drove: Mom and Grandfather and even Dad watching her ride her black-and-white spotted pony, Cookies; stormy nights when Grandfather would sneak her out of bed to watch the lightning from the covered porch; Mom showing her a nest of kittens in the barn. Happy memories that filled her with regret the closer they got to the ranch.

Grandfather had died, and she'd never gone back to see him. He'd been gone two years and she hadn't even known. The news had arrived with the detective hired to track her down and deliver the will. Now the ranch was hers, at least for a short while. This would be her last visit. Best to be rid of it along with all the memories, she told herself. Keeping up with Steph's rock-star lifestyle cost a lot of money, and the realtor had offered a nice sum for the property. What did Renee know about running a ranch, anyway?

The final message in Grandfather's will looped through Renee's mind as she drove.

> The ranch holds a treasure deep under cover
>
> Toliman's secrets are yours to discover
>
> Guard it with care, and love it with spirit
>
> Once you gain their trust, you'll no longer fear it.

Her father would've said it was more of the old man's voodoo or something, putting a poem in a will. But then,

Dad hadn't been invited to the reading, had he? An age-old bitterness rose in Renee's throat. After Mom had died, Dad had shunned Grandfather's "heathen" ways. Something or other about shaman ceremonies and cloven-hoofed devils causing Mom's cancer. The moment Renee'd turned eighteen and inherited Mom's trust fund, she'd run away, thinking only of escaping her father's hysterical recriminations.

Steph thought the poem meant there was buried treasure, and insisted they go check it out before Renee got rid of the place. She'd booked the first available tickets out of La Guardia on Renee's behalf, posting memes about treasure hunting to Instagram and posing for lurking paparazzi with a tiny shovel from one of her previous escapades. "Does it look like I'm ready to dig? Maybe I should shoot a music video while I'm there."

Glancing in the rearview mirror at what was obviously a reporter's car keeping a discreet distance, Renee wondered what fodder they'd end up feeding the ever-hungry press this time. Sometimes she felt like no more than a fictional character of her own life, following Steph around. But living in the rock-star's shadow at least provided an itinerary in Renee's discontented life.

Beneath a gnarled tree in the distance, a herd of dun-colored animals lifted their heads at the SUVs approach. Renee nudged Steph. "Look, elk." At least, she thought they were elk. Maybe deer?

Steph glanced up from her phone, then back down. "Cool. Are we almost there?"

"Soon, I think." Every fencepost they passed along the sage-dotted plateau made Renee's stomach grow tighter and tighter. Why was she so nervous? She felt like something huge was looming on the horizon, a choice she wasn't prepared for, even though her decision to sell had already been made.

The arch of the head gate came into view, Toliman Ranch scrolled in wrought iron along the lintel. She pulled to a stop and opened the car door. A blast of dry heat flooded the air-conditioned cab, along with the far away scent of horses and sunbaked sage brush. She took a deep, appreciative breath, noting the guy behind them hanging from his car window snapping pictures with a telephoto lens. Quickly opening the gate, Renee returned to the cab and the relief of the air conditioner.

"How rustic," Steph said, eyeing the gate as they drove through. "I suppose we have to do that every time we come or go?"

Renee shrugged. "Not so bad. Gave your paparazzi boyfriend an opportunity to flirt with me."

As if in territorial response, Steph rolled down the window and stuck her torso through, offering the cameraman a shot of her ample cleavage. Renee calmly drove past the gate and then hopped back out to shut it behind them. Steph could keep the limelight for all she cared. Renee was a nobody anyway.

She drove another several hundred feet around a hill that blocked most of the house from view of the road. Sunlight danced through motes of dust as they pulled to a stop in front of the wide covered porch. Almost expecting Grandfather to emerge from the house to greet them, she cut the engine.

Steph flung open her door and glanced at Renee with her nose wrinkled. "Whew, what's that smell?"

"Horses," Renee replied, recalling a younger self who'd also wrinkled her nose. Today the smell stirred something in her, as if a trembling bud was about to bloom in her chest. She squashed it down, reminding herself she was only here to hand everything over to the real estate agent. Hopping out, she gazed at the fancy log-frame house with its high windows and country décor. An old rusty wagon wheel hung from the wood shake siding, and the front door fixtures were made of black wrought iron, right down to the old-fashioned knocker shaped like a horse shoe. Two square planter boxes on either edge of the porch steps held nothing but wisps of dry brown grass.

Behind her, the metallic rattle of the barn's bay door opening made her turn. A very tall blonde woman emerged, pointed toes of her cowboy boots impossibly shiny for a ranch worker. The woman raised her chin, as if smelling them as she approached. "Which one of you is Renee?"

Renee stuck out a hand to the giant of a woman, at least giant compared to Renee's five-foot-one frame. "I am."

The woman gripped Renee's knuckles with uncomfortable firmness. "Name's Lori. I've been running the place since your grandfather's death. Sorry for your loss, by the way."

Steph pushed forward, her hand out. "Good to meet you, Lori."

Lori took her hand, eyebrows high. "And you are?"

A look of irritation passed over Steph's features. "Oh, sorry. I'm just so used to being recognized. Steph Bilmore." She cocked her head coyly. "You might have seen one of my music videos?"

"Ah. That would explain the fellow at the gate taking pictures. Hope he knows people in Montana carry guns." The woman turned back to Renee. "How long you planning on staying?"

"Uh," Renee automatically glanced at Steph for validation. "A few days, probably? I've got a realtor coming out tomorrow."

"We're on a treasure hunt," Steph added. "Plus I want to ride a cowboy. I mean a horse." She held up her camera for a selfie next to the wagon wheel on the siding.

Lori's nose flared. "A realtor? I see. Well. The housekeeper's inside. He'll show you your rooms. I'll be in the barn." She spun and strode off without looking back.

Steph sniffed as if unimpressed. "Amazon woman there acts like she owns the place. I suppose we have to get our own luggage, huh?"

"You were a little bold with that cowboy thing," Renee said, feeling strengthened by the Montana air. "We don't even know her."

"This is your property. You can do what you want. She needs to get over herself."

Self-assurance dwindling, Renee nodded and wandered to the fence near the barn, allowing Steph time to sort through her usual mountain of luggage. Leaning against the rough wood rail, Renee surveyed the pasture. Beyond the green, irrigated section within the fence, the rolling hills were calico-spotted with patches of yellow broom and silver-green sagebrush. A shirtless man in a cowboy hat knelt next to one of the sprinkler boxes inside the fence. She admired his broad, tanned back as he picked up and discarded tools and parts. A baby horse with zebra-striped legs pranced around him while its mother grazed placidly nearby.

The man reached a hand behind him while he continued working, wiggling his fingers until the baby nosed them and darted away in delight. The pit of Renee's stomach danced with butterflies watching his obvious affection. The man's throaty laughter floated across the field as he rose and dusted his hands against the front of his jeans. He crouched and did a playful football shuffle, taunting the tiny horse, who kicked up its heels and ran back to its mother.

Momma horse flicked her black tail and continued grazing without concern.

Gathering up his toolbox, the man glanced in Renee's direction, sending the butterflies in her stomach into overdrive. He adjusted his hat off his forehead, letting the sun hit a fine, straight jaw with a haze of stubble. She fluttered her fingers at him, a little thrill chasing down her spine when he lifted a well-muscled arm in a reciprocal greeting. *God, he's hot.* Looking over her shoulder, she realized Steph hadn't yet spotted him. Renee never got the jump on her, often due to her own hesitancy. Well, not today. This was her ranch, and she was going to own it for as long as she could. Heart beating in her throat at her own boldness, she called, "Dibs."

"What?" Steph abandoned the luggage and crunched across the gravel to stand beside her. "Aw, not fair! There'd better be more delicious cowboys around."

Renee grinned. Wow, that felt good. Most of the time, Steph picked the targets and left Renee to play wingman, which meant spending the night fending off the target's wingman. Not this time.

Setting her chin atop her forearms, Renee leaned into the fence, watching the rancher stroll toward the barn. His jeans hugged his lean hips and muscular thighs in exactly the right places, and his muscled abdomen flexed with his gait. He didn't look at her directly, but she could feel his attention igniting her core.

Face heating, she looked away.

Steph turned back to the car. "If you don't seal the deal before tomorrow, all dibs are off."

Her previous thrill of confidence crumbled. "Hey! I called dibs!"

"Dibs are first shot, not exclusive. So don't screw it up. Just screw." Steph smirked and rattled her wheeled suitcase across the gravel into the house.

Yanking her own suitcase from the jumbled pile of Steph's castoffs, Renee scurried after her.

lack's ears rang from the conversation between the two women as he entered the barn. They had no way of knowing he could hear them that far away—no human could, at least not clearly. The tiny brunette with the pixie face looked damned sexy peeking over the top fence rail at him, and she smelled amazing even at this distance, like wind coming off a cherry orchard in bloom. The other one wasn't bad, either, but she had a hard scent about her that reminded him of a predator.

He set his toolbox just inside the barn, safely away from little Ivy-Jane's curious mouth, and, now that he was out of sight of the ladies, he adjusted his fly. How long had it been since he'd had a woman? According to his hardening dick, too long. There weren't a lot of options for a centaur living on a remote ranch. To the herd he was a misshapen monster, unable to assume full equine form, and to humans, a monster of myth. Centaurs had no place in either world.

He headed to the back corner stall where they stored extra parts and equipment for the hinky water system that served the ranch. Parts of the system dated back over a hundred years. The water outlet had been clogged with rust, and he hoped they had a spare O-ring.

Should he approach the brunette or let her come to him? Young stallions from the herd hooked up with humans at the local bar occasionally, but that outlet had been quashed when Lori took over. She enforced strict rules over who left the ranch and for what purpose, minimizing what she called "frivolous" interactions with humans.

The image of the little pixie, small breasts pressed against the middle fence rung while she watched him, wouldn't leave him. Oh, how he'd love to get frivolous with that. To nuzzle into the warm curve of her neck while she wrapped both legs around him. His dick hardened even more at the thought. Good thing there was no one around right now.

He dug through a plastic bucket of miscellaneous-sized O-rings, comparing the old one from the spigot for size. Lori wanted the ranch—the entire plateau, for that matter—as a haven for shifters. No humans at all, even though Old Man Toliman had known about the herd and provided things like medical assistance and winter forage. With him gone, the herd was on shaky ground.

The scuffing of feet against the dirt floor behind him made him look over his shoulder. The Lead Mare leaned against the doorway, one boot crossed over the other. "I have a job for you, soldier."

He went back to digging through the bucket, dick thankfully shriveling at her presence. He hated her nickname for him, as if he only lived to follow her orders, not be part of the herd he protected. "I'm already working on something."

"You heard we have visitors."

He shrugged one shoulder noncommittally.

"The midget is Toliman's heir. I need you to marry her. The sooner the better."

Bristling, he shoved the parts bucket back onto its shelf and turned. "Marry her? I thought you wanted nothing to do with humans?"

Lori lowered her chin, brown eyes flashing with authority. Sometimes he wondered if her sire had been a wild cat instead of a stallion to give her the kind of command she seemed to wield. She spoke in a sultry tenor that brooked no argument. "She's got a realtor coming. One of us needs to marry in, take ownership. Keep her from selling the place or turning it into a tourist trap."

"Why me?" He exited the storage stall, brushing uncomfortably close to her when she refused to step aside.

"You're here at the barn more than any of the others. And it's not like you fucking a human could pollute the bloodlines any worse than you already have." She followed at his heels, her voice close to his ear. His skin crawled as if she might nip his flank any moment. He hated it when she tried to pull herd rank on him in human form. "You're probably already half-hard thinking about mounting her, anyway. Do it. I'll tell the other stallions to back off. Just watch out for that friend of hers. She's a piece of work."

"Mounting's one thing. Marrying's another."

Did she think Toliman's granddaughter would simply marry a strange ranch hand and sign things over? He bent to pick up the toolbox. "Old Man Toliman kept our secret for decades. Why don't we just tell his granddaughter?"

Lori stepped so close to him, their boots touched. "Not one word. Our secret died with that old man and it better stay that way."

A direct order? How was he supposed to build trust strong enough to propose marriage to a human, yet keep that kind of secret? He dropped his gaze, lip curling with distaste at Lori's nearness, and backed up a step. "You expect me to just drop to one knee and propose out of the blue? I have a feeling she's smarter than that."

"I've seen you in action at the bar, soldier. I know you'll make her swoon. Convince her to be your bride, and I'll ensure you have a place in the herd. A real place, running the wind with the rest of us."

The idea took hold of him like a lover's hand cupping his balls. He'd dreamed of running with the herd since before his first shift at seventeen. Unlike other equine shifters, he'd been born to his mother while she was in human form—a human baby—and had endured his long childhood waiting for his first shift to join his grandmother's herd. As time wore on, and he'd shown no sign of the ability, everyone assumed it would never happen. He'd tried so hard to make it happen, when it finally did... Well, he'd nearly killed himself shifting over and over in an attempt to "get it right."

He never could.

The herd hadn't exactly shunned him—they didn't dare when his grandmother was the Lead Mare. But the indulgence they'd once shown the poor human boy, like bareback rides across the plateau, had quickly turned to disdain and dismissal. The entire reason he'd gone to vet school was to give himself worth to the herd. But even that hadn't increased his rank. Being a vet was a human thing.

He licked his lips, regarding Lori warily. "How do you propose to make the herd take me in when I can't even run with them?"

She lowered her chin to stare him down. "What I say, goes. You know that. Once we own the ranch, you'll be free to roam like never before. And if you don't do it, I can find someone who will."

His heart palpitated in an uncomfortable rhythm. He'd never considered himself marriageable. But to belong to a herd, he'd do almost anything. And either way, Toliman's granddaughter was a tempting treat. "If I pull this off, and she becomes my little ranch wife, how're you going to hide our secret then?"

Lori's grin was feral as she retreated into the barn. "Believe me, she won't stick around."

Black was suddenly sick to his stomach as he considered what Lori might mean.

*R*enee stared at the huge barn door and swallowed. Steph was in the house, tied to a wall phone so she could talk to her agent. Cell service apparently didn't reach the ranch. But this gave Renee an opportunity to find that cowboy without Steph's watchful judgment or a teasing recap of her clumsy flirting later.

Why does it have to be so damn hot? She held her arms away from her body, hoping for a cooling breeze. Despite a reapplication of antiperspirant, her underarms were already stained with sweat.

Taking a deep breath, she ventured into the barn, hoping she'd find him there. She peered down the length of stalls, refamiliarizing herself with a layout she faintly remembered from childhood. The stalls to the right were simple, chain-link cubicles, while the ones to the left were enclosed in solid wood. The empty barn echoed, the sweet scent of warm hay and dust permeating the air. A bare-bones wooden stairway climbed into the hay loft, while several bales of straw formed a more solid looking stairway of their own at the other end of the building.

What if he's not here? Or worse, what if he's already involved with that Lori chick? She clutched what little confidence she had left tightly within her and ventured into the barn's cool, dim interior. "Hello?"

The man in the cowboy hat appeared from behind the straw stairway, now wearing a dark, form-fitting tee shirt. *What a shame.* At least his shoulders and biceps stretched the fabric in all the right places. An arrow of sweat darkened the shirt's neckline, pointing down between his sculpted pecs.

He strolled toward her, well-worn cowboy boots scuffing against the hay-strewn floor, each step sending quivers through her core. He had a strong jaw dusted with five o'clock shadow, dusky blond hair curled slightly over his ears, strong, straight nose, and sensual lips. Under his mahogany gaze, her pussy felt anxious, hot, and undeniably wet.

"You must be the new owner." His voice was as low and sexy as she'd imagined.

If she wanted to beat Steph at dibs, she'd need to play like Steph. *Say something sexy.* But all she could think of was riding a cowboy. Totally inappropriate. Instead, she smiled and stuck out a hand. "Howdy partner!"

Howdy partner? Really? That was the best she could come up with? She shook her head and said a small prayer that her blush was invisible in the dim light of the barn. He accepted her handshake, his large, work-calloused grip firm but in no way uncomfortable. In fact, the contact sent a delightful shiver up her arm as she imagined that hand touching other parts of her skin.

She cleared her throat and tried again. "My name's Renee. What's yours?"

A tiny smile twitched at one corner of his mouth, and she was drawn into his warm brown gaze. "Black."

"Black? That's your first name?"

"Yep." His gaze flicked down to their still-clasped hands.

She scrambled for a Steph-like quip to keep the ball rolling. "Let me guess. Black Beauty?" *Oh, God, what was she doing? A little girl's book? Come on, Renee.* "No, too girly. Black Jack? No, that's a pirate." *Bad to worse...* "Oh, wait, Black Stallion!" Her blush built to an almost intolerable heat, and she was dying to cover her face with both hands. Then she realized she was still clutching his hand. She jerked free, trying to stand tall when all she wanted to do was cringe.

The twitch at the corner of his mouth rose to a full smile. "Close. Black Stevens."

Before he could say more, Lori emerged from one of the wood stalls behind him. The tall woman clapped a hand to his shoulder, but not with what Renee would call affection. More like possessiveness. "I see you've met our ranch-hand. Black here's been assigned to show you around."

Rats. He *was* taken. It figured that the one time Renee'd claimed dibs on a hot guy, she'd choose one who was already hitched.

Shrugging off Lori's grip, Black scowled and turned to look at her. "You and I need to talk about that."

"You can always go back to mucking out stalls." Lori's smile was tight.

Renee held both palms out. There was some serious tension going on, and she did not want to get in the middle of it. "Hey, I don't want to interrupt a lover's quarrel. I can come back later."

Black let out a rough laugh. "Lori and I are not, and never will be, lovers."

The tall woman's haughty expression confirmed his words. Whatever was going on between these two had nothing to do with sex. Unsure what to make of things, Renee looked around to find a new subject. "I don't suppose Cookies is still here? Grandfather used to keep a pony for me."

Lori laughed. "No Cookies for you, my dear." She shot a strange glance toward Black. "I'll arrange to saddle our stallion, Saul for you."

Black seemed to stiffen. "Saddle Saul? What's Saul think of that?"

With a disdainful look, Lori moved past him toward Renee. "He's eager to please."

Black turned as she walked by. Cleared his throat. Shifted to address Renee. "A stallion might be a bit much for you."

"Nonsense." Lori flicked a hand dismissively, sending lazy dust motes into a swirling frenzy. "She's Toliman's granddaughter. I mean, look at her. She's got the curve-less physique of a jockey. Plus, I hear she and her friend are thrill-seekers. Saul's going to love her."

Tension permeated the barn, loaded with a subtext Renee couldn't fathom. Steph loved the hype of thrill-seeking for her paparazzi, but in truth, the things Steph did scared the bejesus out of Renee. Riding a stallion sounded like it might be right up there with swimming in a shark cage. Besides, Grandfather had died riding a horse, and she was nowhere near as skilled as he'd been. "Er, I haven't been on a horse since I was eight."

Black grabbed Renee's arm and turned her firmly toward one of the stalls open to the pasture. "Why don't I show you around before you decide anything? Let's save the riding for later, when it's not so hot." He shot a look over his shoulder but didn't slow down. "We have a new foal. She was just born a few days ago."

"Sounds good," Renee said breathlessly, dodging a drying pile of manure.

"Let me know how you enjoy riding!" Lori's voice floated after them, followed by a laugh.

Now that they were away from Lori, Renee tilted her head to check out Black's jeans-covered ass. Not too baggy, not too full. *Nice.* She trailed her gaze up his broad back to the sexy muss of hair peeking from beneath his cowboy hat. Were all cowboy hats called Stetsons, or was that a specific brand?

A loose rock twisted under her foot, causing her to lurch forward. He spun and caught her by both arms before she fell. *Ohh, quick* and *strong.* She smiled coyly up into his face, pleased at the startled blink he gave her before he looked away. *See, this Steph thing's not so hard. Well, as long as no talking was required...*

"Careful," he said. "These rocks seem to appear out of nowhere." He turned and continued walking, no longer holding Renee's arm. *Shucks.* She closed her eyes and inhaled the lingering scent of him. Sweet hay and leather and sexy, sexy man.

Opening her eyes again, she was abashed to see him looking at her from a few steps away, near the mare. A smirk tweaked his sensual lips. "This is Millie."

The mare cocked her ears toward Renee curiously.

Cheeks burning, Renee straightened her spine and held out a hand to the horse as if to shake. "Good to meet you, Millie. I'm Renee." *There, that was cute, right?* The beast bobbed her head as if in greeting, and Renee giggled and curtsied back, pleased by Black's approving smile. "So polite!"

"Millie, Renee's the new owner of the ranch, and she'd like to meet Ivy-Jane if you don't mind."

The tiny foal peeked out from behind its mom's hindquarters, nose too big for her body and dainty feet ringed with stripes. Renee let out a gust of air. "Oh, my, God, she's adorable."

The foal startled back into hiding. Momma horse flicked her tail and turned around to continue grazing, as if shrugging in acquiescence.

Black crouched and leaned forward, offering one hand toward where the foal had disappeared. "It's okay, Ivy-Jane. Come meet the human."

Renee admired his wide chest as he stretched his arm. "I like how you talk to them."

He rose without looking at her. "It's about respect, that's all. Isn't it, Millie?" He scratched the mare's neck where her dark mane emerged. "And with the little ones, you need to allow them to come to you. They can sense who to trust."

The foal peeked at them again, this time from around the mare's front end, dark ears back. Renee averted her eyes, keeping focus on Black. Not difficult to do. The muscles in his forearm rippled as he scratched the mare, and the tiny gold hairs on his skin caught the sun. Remembering how he'd stretched a teasing hand out to the foal while he was working on the sprinkler box, Renee held her palm up and wiggled her fingers at the foal.

To her delight, the little creature approached to sniff, velvet muzzle brushing the backs of Renee's fingers.

"Seems you pass muster." Black watched with a hooded gaze and easy smile. Damn, he had a sexy smile.

"How old are they when you start breaking them?"

Millie nickered and swished her tail, sending the little foal skittering away before turning and plodding slowly after. Renee let her arm drop in disappointment.

"We don't break horses here." Black's voice held a low growl of irritation. The hooded smile had transformed to stone. "Besides, Millie's... from the wild herd."

"Sorry. I meant tame." Renee raised her brows, but his face didn't soften. "Work with? I don't know horse lingo. Besides, I thought wild horses would run away. Why's she in your pasture?"

Black removed his hat and ran a hand over his dusty blond curls. "Old Man Toliman—your grandfather— always helped horses. Didn't matter if they were his, the neighbors', or from the wild herd. He offered protection for new foals. Provided forage during hard winters. Medical help when needed." He shrugged. "We try to honor his methods."

More of that wistful sensation that had captured her on the drive here, that sense of something lost, took hold of her. She had a vivid image of her grandfather's broad smile whenever he took her out to the barn or pasture. "He used to pull me around in a little wagon to see all the horses. He'd say we were going visiting," she said, tears filming her eyes. Why had she never come back here to visit? Just because Dad was worried about voodoo or some such? "Grandfather loved horses."

A breeze passed between her and Black like a ghost, and she wiped her eyes with the backs of her hands. She tried to laugh. "Sorry."

Black's rich mahogany gaze sought hers. The stony face he'd worn earlier had softened yet remained serious, like he was expecting something of her. "Maybe you can love horses, too."

She laughed again, heart pounding like a flighty bird in her chest. Mr. Intense was one compelling fellow. She shifted her gaze back toward the barn. If anyone could make her love horses again, it would be Black Stevens.

"Maybe you can take me riding and show me how?" She tilted her head and shot him that same shy, coy look she had when she'd tripped on the rock. Her nethers tingled with the desire to ride, and not necessarily a horse.

He breathed in deeply, as if absorbing her. "Sure."

"Oh!" She remembered Grandfather's poem. "And Grandfather's will said something about buried treasure. You heard anything about that?"

"Uh... nope."

"Well, you're officially recruited to help look for it." She took his work-calloused hand and pulled him back toward the barn to saddle some horses, her forced boldness making her heart flutter.

4

*W*ith utter bemusement, Black allowed the pixie to lead him back to the barn. He was supposed to be seducing her, not the other way around. How the hell was he supposed to think straight when he was continually fighting a hard-on near her? He'd never had this kind of physical reaction around anyone. It was as if his body was hyper aware of her every move. When she'd stumbled on that rock, that look she'd given him, electric and inviting, had just about knocked him flat on his back.

Just because she's flirting doesn't mean she's looking for anything permanent.

She was likely after a vacation fling. Which he'd be happy to oblige, except for Lori's scheme. And threats.

First of all, it didn't sound like she intended there to be a happily-ever-after marriage, which is why Black had hesitated during Renee's introduction. Then there was the other threat, almost as sour as the first. *If you don't do it, I can find someone who will.* Someone like Saul, who was more than a stallion—he was Black's Uncle Saul, the leader of the Bachelor herd.

The idea of Saul mounting Renee—or the other way around, for that matter—made Black's hands curl into fists. Not that Uncle Saul was a bad guy, but the thought of anyone besides himself riding that sweet little filly made him want to punch someone.

The barn's cool shadow enveloped them and Renee let out an audible breath. She plucked at her tee shirt, exposing a glimpse of her lacy pink bra and sending out wafts of her amazing cherry-blossom scent, like a cool spring breeze on a sweltering summer day. *Get it together, Black. You're acting like a yearling around a mare in heat.*

"Damn, that sun's hot," Renee said in a breathy voice, sexy as hell. "I don't know how you work in it all day."

He let his gaze wander from her face to her breasts and lower, then back up to meet her eyes, nostrils twitching with her intoxicating aroma. "What's that perfume you're wearing?"

She flushed. "Just deodorant."

He liked the way he could make her blush. She was a good girl trying to be bad, and he had to admit it was appealing as hell. Wanting to see just how pink she could get, he took a deep, purposeful breath. "You smell delicious."

Her flush deepened and she shifted her gaze away shyly.

The strength of his cock surged against the hard zipper on his jeans. He stepped forward until he was sure she could feel his breath on her skin. He was sure he smelled of horse and sweat, but Renee didn't seem to mind. In fact, she seemed drawn to it, if her earlier nose-to-the-wind moment was any indication.

She tilted her chin to look up at him, the flush of embarrassment melting into an aroused glow. Her lashes fluttered closed, lips parted slightly, ready for him to taste.

Much as he wanted to throw her into the hay and sink himself inside her, he knew he had to do more. He had to win her heart. He'd never played at courting before, because no mare would ever choose a centaur. His previous sexual encounters had always been with humans, quick and dirty, no tethers attached. And now here was Renee, offering him the usual steamy interlude, and he was thinking about bonding.

"You ever been in love?" His voice was husky in his own ears.

Her eyes popped open. A flash of something vulnerable passed through her gaze. Then the wild filly was back. She reached up to run her index finger from his throat down his chest. "What a silly question."

He reached up and grabbed her hand, stilling it against his breastbone. Her heated skin was soft. Looking deeply into her eyes, he said, "I take that to mean 'no.'"

There it was again, that vulnerable flash behind her eyes. She straightened her spine. "This doesn't have to be about love. We can just have some fun."

He frowned back. Behind her clumsy attempts at flirting he'd glimpsed someone worthy of being Toliman's granddaughter. Someone capable of love. Not a woman on the prowl. He rubbed his thumb across the soft skin of her palm. "You don't want more?"

She shook her head. "Love's just a way to get yourself killed, if not in body, then in spirit. I watched my dad turn into a stranger after Mom died." She shook her head, as if flinging away memories. "I'm not looking for love."

Black raised a brow at her, knowing he was about to push some buttons. But he wanted to know who he was really dealing with. "So you decided to become a player, instead? A predator?"

She blinked. Pulled her hand free. But he caught it and brought it back to his chest. She glared up at him. "I'm not a player."

In that moment, something about her posture, the way she defended herself, grabbed hold of his heart's reins. This little blushing filly was definitely not a predator. Pretending to be, maybe, but when push came to shove, she wasn't the type to leave a string of broken hearts behind her. No, this one was playing a game, like a yearling flirting with a new herd.

He gave her a wry smile. "If you're not a player, then you're a tease."

She gasped and jerked her hand free. "I'm not a tease!"

"No?" He stepped closer, pressing his chest against hers, forcing her to back up. One step, two, until she bumped the post he'd been aiming her toward. "Prove it."

He looked down into her wide eyes, and when she didn't push him away, he ducked his head to meet her lips. Cupping one side of her head, he threaded his fingers into her pixie hair. The softness of her mouth, the sweet flavor as she opened to him, made his head reel. She seemed to melt beneath him, opening up like petals to the sun. Her hands slipped to his hipbones, sending shivers across his skin, igniting his already rock-hard cock. Damn, this woman was like a drug.

He found himself kissing her harder, slipping his tongue between her teeth. Exploring her mouth. Inhaling her breath as his own.

She arched her breasts against him, throwing her head back and exposing her neck. He nibbled along her jawline, his hat bumping her cheek. She reached up and knocked it tumbling to the floor. Freed, he pulled her tightly against him and dropped his mouth to the sensitive skin at the curve of her neck. Her warm scent engulfed him, deeply female and exciting. Her nipples had risen like little buttons through her shirt, prodding him through the fabric. God, he wanted to taste those breasts.

She set both hands at the back of his hips and rolled herself against him, grinding his erection into her. He reached down and cupped her backside, lifting her slightly, fitting her to him. She made a tiny noise at the back of her throat that about sent him over the edge. Her hands roamed his back, his sides, swept down to rummage for the hem of his shirt and slide beneath, burn trails across his skin as she stroked his abs and sought his own hardened nipples.

"Woohoo, you go girl!" A flash penetrated his closed eyelids, and a familiar, predatory scent intruded on the moment. "This is so going on your Instagram page."

Renee stiffened, her fingers ceasing their caress. He loosed his grip, turning to face their peeping Tom while stepping between Renee and the camera. Her friend stood there in a low-cut tanktop, Daisy-Dukes, and flip flops, her frosted hair falling in two short braids to either side of her face. He growled, "What are you doing?"

"Capturing the moment." Steph didn't look up from her phone as she typed something to go with the photo.

He lowered his chin to glare at her. Photos were something he avoided, for obvious reasons. "You shouldn't publicize pictures of people you don't know."

She looked up to meet his gaze with artful innocence. "Oh, we're definitely getting to know you. Aren't we, Renee? Besides, I told that fellow out at the gate he could come inside with his camera."

"You did what?" His hands balled into fists. His head felt naked without his hat, and he searched the dirt floor until he found it. Dusting it against his knee, he glared at her. "We tend to be private here at the ranch."

"You have nothing to be ashamed of, stud muffin. You are one gorgeous hunk of man!" She grinned and snapped another photo of him.

Gritting his teeth, he slapped his hat back onto his head, taking one step toward her. He was going to yank the phone right out of her grasp and—

Renee's soft touch on his arm reined him in. He crossed his arms and waited to see what his little filly would do.

*R*enee stepped out from behind Black, trying to calm her racing pulse. Steph was just being Steph, taking over like she owned the place. Only this time, Renee actually did own the place. This was Renee's territory, and for once she had no patience for Steph's disrespect. "Steph, not everyone wants their life out in the open."

"Don't worry, the photos didn't post. I don't have cell service here. This place is so backwater." She shoved the phone into her back pocket. "I came to tell you we've been invited to go base jumping! We're leaving for Dubai in the morning. Let's get this treasure hunting thing out of the way and move on." She looked around as if the treasure might pop out of hiding any moment.

"Base jumping?" Renee's step faltered. Steph had been talking about base jumping for almost a year. She'd even convinced Renee to do a tandem parachute jump in "preparation." Renee had sprained an ankle and been laid up for over a week.

"There's this building there, like, a million miles high. People do it all the time. And if we get caught, we could end up in prison." Steph squealed and made a little mock face of excited fear.

Black's deep voice rumbled at Renee's back. "You're excited to go to prison in Dubai?"

"Oh, we won't end up in prison. At least not for long. I've got people to get me out."

"And what about Renee?" His voice was hard as iron. Renee wasn't sure if that made her feel worried or safe. He was looking out for her, but his animosity toward Steph was almost physical.

Steph moved around Renee toward him, a familiar hungry glint in her eye. "Aw, that's so sweet, I love a man who's protective."

"Dibs, remember?" Renee gritted softly between her teeth.

Huffing, Steph spun and flounced toward the bay doors. "We don't have time, anyway. We have to be in Dubai day after tomorrow. Jamison has it all arranged."

"That's not enough time." Renee swallowed, trying to find some courage—not courage to base jump. No way in hell she was doing that. She needed courage to tell Steph no.

"You haven't signed the papers yet, so everything'll still be here when we get back. Maybe your lover-boy can find a friend for me while we're gone?" Steph shot a look over her shoulder at Black, pursing her lips in a playful kiss. "Come on, Renee."

Renee gave Black a tight smile. The set of his shoulders told her his hackles were still up. Best she step away and deal with Steph now. "I'll have to take you up on that ride later."

Scurrying after her friend, she caught up in the gravel lot where they'd parked the Ford. Steph had the back end open and was digging through one of the suitcases. "I'm sure I packed my Louis Vuitton flats in here. I want to wear them on the plane."

"We just got here, Steph. I want to stay a few days." Renee paused beside the SUV to watch Steph unfold and refold several stacks of clothing, all too fancy for the ranch.

"This jump is a once in a lifetime chance." Steph didn't look up. "You don't want to miss it."

Renee swallowed, her stomach churning. "I have an appointment with the realtor. Why don't you go on without me? Maybe I can catch up?"

"Is this about the money?" Steph scowled. "You know I'll cover you until you can pay me back."

"No, it's not that. I just want to get this ranch thing handled."

Steph paused her assessment of a navy blue sleeveless blouse dotted with sequins and looked at Renee. "Renee." She tossed the blouse on top of the open suitcase. "Are you really going to flake on me now, when I've finally lined this up? You know I've been waiting months for this."

At the edge of the barn, Renee spotted the glint of a camera lens as the paparazzi took his opportunity. Rolling her eyes, she redirected her attention to Steph. "You'll have Jamison. Anyway, three's a crowd."

"He has a friend for you, too. Not like here, where *I'm* the third wheel." She wrinkled her nose like a petulant child.

"I haven't been here since I was eight, and I've barely had a look around—"

"Come on! It'll be a blast! The shopping in Dubai is crazy."

Renee shrugged one shoulder, trying to keep the acid in her stomach from rising any farther into her throat. "I think I'm going to stay here." There. She'd said it.

Steph squinted at her, her lash extensions shading her flecked green eyes. Her scrutiny shifted to the barn and back again, not even acknowledging the camera guy there. "I see. Thrown over for a penis."

"What? I would never—"

"What do you call it, then?"

Renee swallowed back the sour taste filling her mouth, her blood pumping as hard now as it had while kissing Black. Truth was, she *did* want to stay and see where things went with him. Plus, the ranch was bringing back so many memories, she felt she needed some time to absorb them before the ranch was no longer hers. Black was helping her do that in a way that felt safe. Like she could be herself instead of the player she had to act like in Steph's shadow. Renee dug her nails into her palms. "I don't want to go base jumping. Not now, not ever."

Her friend's eyes widened and she took a half step back, as if she'd been slapped. "Oh. Well, why didn't you say so?"

Eyes burning with angry tears, Renee shook her head. "I
—you—" The words were choking her, too many held
back for too long.

Steph reached out to pull Renee into a hug. "I know, I
know. You just did." She squeezed until Renee's hands
rose to hug her back. "Fine. I'll go by myself. I already
told my fans. But don't sell this place until I get back. We
have a treasure to find."

Renee slumped against Steph in relief, guilt already
sprouting in her chest, urging her to relent. To pack up
and go back to being Steph's shadow. Instead, she simply
said, "Thank you."

Planting a big kiss on Renee's cheek, Steph said, "Make
sure to take notes on that juicy cowboy. I'm going to
want all the deets."

Renee gave her a wry grin. Then she pointed to the
paparazzi skulking beside the barn. "Meanwhile, can you
get rid of your boyfriend over there?"

5

*B*lack stomped back to the barn to grab a bridle for Petunia, resenting the need to rely on a normal horse's legs to carry him, but he couldn't shift with all these humans about. And the herd needed to know right away about the photographer before one of them got careless and shifted near the barn. On top of that, the mention of a realtor proved Lori really did have a reason for him to move fast with Renee. Developers had been hounding Toliman to sell for years, but the old man had held out, mostly because of the herd. Without the ranch, they'd no longer be able to *be* a herd.

Whether Black married Renee or found another way to convince her to keep the property, he had to do it soon.

A thump from the stall where they stored grain and medical supplies drew his attention. *Too loud to be a barn cat.* Had one of the ranch's yearlings snuck in to get into the grain again? He didn't need a colicky horse added to his list of worries. It didn't rain, it poured, as the saying went. He sighed and grabbed the nearest bridle before going to check it out.

Around the corner, near the shelves of vet supplies, stood a man with his back to the door. His shirtless torso showed the many years of tiny scars his position as Lead Bachelor had gained him from nips and kicks as he jostled for dominance.

"Uncle Saul?"

The dark-haired man swung around, holding a bloody swath of gauze. A fresh magenta bruise stained his cheekbone.

"What happened?" Black moved forward.

"Eh, I'm fine. Lori caught me with a hoof, that's all." He was favoring his right arm, and blood smeared his ribs.

"She do this to you before or after she volunteered you as a steed?" Rage burned the back of Black's throat. Shifters only offered that honor to very special humans. Like his grandma and Old Man Toliman. They'd run the ranch together as if they were an old married couple, and she'd often served as his steed. But that was her choice. Not even the Lead Mare had a right to force another herd member to serve as a mount.

"This had nothing to do with that." Still favoring his arm, Saul grabbed a shirt from one of the wall pegs and started to put it on.

"Wait. Let me take a look." Black strode forward to examine the laceration on his uncle's ribs. The sharp edge of an unshod hoof had left a gash surrounded by bruising that might hint at broken bones. "How's your breathing?"

"I'll recover." Saul's voice carried a thread of pain that showed even through his gruffness. He tended to overdo the alpha posturing, especially in human form. After a decade leading the other bachelors, his position had become a point of pride for him. "Just have to take it easy."

"You're Lead Bachelor, not some gelding." Black searched for a bottle of antiseptic spray on the shelves. "She had no right to do this."

"She caught Grant in the canyon after she told everyone to stay out. Went after him like she does. He's just a kid, so I stepped in. Things got a little rough."

Black frowned. "Grant's okay?"

Saul nodded tersely.

"Why's she keeping the herd out of the canyon?" The canyon provided shade and sometimes pockets of water or green grass during the drought of summer. It was also a nice place to hide from tourist eyes and allow young shifters a chance to master their human form. Black had enjoyed the relative solitude many times in his centaur form.

"Says it's cursed ground since we lost both Gloryanna and Old Man Toliman there."

"I see." Black located the bottle and leveled the nozzle at Saul's wound. Toliman had been riding Black's grandmother—Saul's mother—when the accident happened. The official report said icy rocks and a trail too close to the edge had fouled up the older horse's footing and plummeted both horse and rider to their deaths. Lori declared it'd been the old mare giving her human one last ride. Black still had difficulty believing his grandma would've been on that trail under those conditions.

He finished cleaning the blood from Saul's side and reached for a laceration kit. "You're going to need a couple stitches."

"Naw, it's okay." Saul stuffed an arm into his sleeve.

"I insist." Black glowered at his uncle. "You may outrank me on the range, but in here, I'm the vet. You need stitches."

Saul paused, eyes swinging to meet Black's. After one blink, he dropped his gaze in acquiescence. He pulled his shirt loose and exposed his side once again. "All right, then."

Black's heartbeat slowed a little. He hated these battles for hierarchy. He'd prefer a more democratic way of interacting with his brethren. But instincts ran strong, and traditions were hard to overcome. He broke out a sterile needle and pinched the gaping skin together to begin the first stitch. "Uncle Saul, you ever hear anything about a buried treasure around here?"

Saul twitched as the needle entered his skin. "Buried treasure? Like pirates or something?"

"Not sure. Renee—Toliman's granddaughter—said there was something in the will about a buried treasure."

Saul's laugh forced Black to pause or risk skewering his uncle in the wrong spot. "I don't think your grandmother expected that one."

"Huh?"

"Toliman wanted to tell his granddaughter about us, but the girl never came to visit. And you know our policy about putting any of our history in writing. Gloryanna convinced the herd advisors to let him put a cutesy poem in the will."

"So the treasure is... the herd?"

"Hidden, not buried. And yes, I believe so."

Black tugged the stitch tight and tied it off. "Renee's in for a surprise, then."

"Only if she discovers us."

"If Toliman wanted her to know, we should tell her."

Saul turned to face his nephew. "Lori wants to keep humans out of herd business."

Black surveyed his uncle's swollen eye. "You're head of the Bachelor Herd. What do you think about it?"

Shoving his head into his shirt, Saul grunted. "Doesn't matter what I think. It's a herd thing."

The underlying subtext—that Black wasn't part of the herd and couldn't understand—stung. Lori's promise to give Black a place in the hierarchy felt like an impossible dream when even his own uncle couldn't accept him. Black held up the needle. "You need one more stitch."

"Not unless you want me to kick you." With that, Saul stalked out the door.

That night Renee and Steph had a bonfire, staying up far too late and drinking far too much tequila. She glimpsed Black watching from the barn door, but he chose not to join the bonfire, and she was grateful. She didn't want to share him with Steph. There would be plenty of time tomorrow to flirt with her cowboy.

Steph stumbled to bed slobbery and emotional about leaving Renee behind. Renee fell asleep dreaming about cowboys and adventures that were all her own. The next morning she woke woefully hung over, but managed to see Steph off before stumbling back to bed. Around noon she woke again, suddenly alert to the fact she was on her own. No one else was going to decide where to go or what to do. It was all up to her. Today was going to be fantastic. She just knew it.

Jumping out of bed, she stretched and smiled, gazing from her second story window across the rolling grasslands. Heat waves shimmered the air outside, giving the day a dream-like quality. After showering, Renee dressed in light capris and a strappy tank-top with a forget-me-not appliqué and matching sandals. She blotted her face, and applied a light coat of lipstick, then headed into the afternoon sunlight to find her sexy cowboy. Flirting with Black felt like uncharted territory without Steph's looming presence.

She found Black in the pasture once again working on the sprinkler head, this time with a shirt on. He looked up as she crossed the gravel parking area. Putting on what she thought was a sassy smile, she opened the gate and entered, keeping an eye out for rocks. A slight breeze had picked up, and the sun cast long golden shadows through the tufts of grass.

"I'm ready for a ride." She immediately kicked herself. *Stop trying so hard.*

He looked her head to toe with an appreciative gaze, lingering on her breasts and hips in a way that heated her already-flushed skin. His attention drifted back down to her strappy little sandals. "You planning to ride in those?"

"Why not? They're cute, right?" She stopped a few feet away and wiggled her sparkly red toenails at him. She knew riding in sandals was a bad idea, but she wasn't trying to impress a horse.

"At least you're not in Daisy Dukes." He rose. "Not that I'd mind ogling your legs. But that'd be begging for saddle burn. C'mon, I have a spare set of boots in the barn."

He put a familiar hand at the small of her back and led her to the barn. The contact seemed to draw energy from his hand, sending tingles over her hips and spine as they walked. He ducked into a stall holding odds and ends and reappeared with a dusty pair of leather cowboy boots.

Nerve endings crying out at the break in contact, she eyed the footwear. Steph had a policy about sharing footwear; shoes carried toenail fungus. Renee didn't know if that was true, but why risk it? "I'm not wearing used boots."

"You need heels to stick in the stirrups." He thrust the boots forward.

What would he do if she put her foot down? She didn't really care about riding a horse at the moment. Trying to be cute, she pursed her lips. "I have a pair of stilettos in my suitcase. I could wear those."

His eyes narrowed and his mouth quirked into a smile. "You can wear those with your Daisy Dukes later."

She blushed, legs going rubbery, the churning sensation low in her belly distracting her. *You walked right into that one.* He was good at putting images in her head. Her, in stilettos, backed against the barn post while he pushed aside the crotch of her short shorts to...

Black's nostrils flared slightly, and his playful expression shifted intensity. He advanced, and her heart kicked up a notch, his leather and sweet-hay scent filling her senses. Heat flooded her panties. She backed up a step, wad of hay catching the lip of one sandal and making her wobble. His arm shot out to steady her. A nuclear jolt of energy coursed up her arm. She closed her eyes and leaned into him, allowing the sensation to wash over her.

To her surprise, he pressed the boots into her grip and backed away. "If you want to ride, you need to wear boots."

She opened her eyes, her gaze on the worn leather in her hands. "Even for a short ride?"

"You wanted to look for buried treasure, so we're going camping."

Another memory of her grandfather surfaced, of nights sleeping under a sky milky with stars, crickets singing her to sleep. "I haven't been camping in ages."

"I've got the gear all packed." He turned toward the length of stalls.

Her excitement twisted into a new kind of anticipation, rapid heartbeat making her dizzy. "You know where the treasure is?"

"I have some ideas." He clicked his tongue and a dark speckled muzzle appeared over the stall door. "This is Petunia. She'll be your mount today."

Thinking back to Lori's earlier offer, she teased, "I'll be riding a stallion in no time."

Black turned toward her slowly, his eyes narrowed to mahogany slits and a wicked smile curving his lips. "You will. And I'm going to make sure you're good and ready."

All rational thought flooded from her head and pooled with scorching intensity at the apex of her thighs. *Good God, how'd he do that?* She'd been offering crappy innuendos all day, and here he'd thrown her off balance with a single zinger. *What would Steph do?* She widened her stance and lifted her chin. "I make that decision."

His voice went silken, deep with promise. "And how will you decide which stallion to ride?"

She swallowed as he paced forward, his gaze boring into her. The swell in his jeans told her he was ready, even if she was now weak in the knees. When he reached her, he paused, eyes shifting downward to her lips, throat, then breasts. She could scarcely breathe. He eased sideways, eyes devouring her. Maintaining that intangible connection, he moved around her, so close she could feel his breath on her skin. She craned her neck to follow him, keeping the rest of her body frozen in place.

His warmth stopped moving behind her. A hand gripped her neck, fingers threading into the hair at the base of her skull. Pressing slightly, he drew her head down and to the side. Breath heated her neck as he grazed his chin over the curve of her shoulder, trailing his mouth over her sensitive flesh. He paused, sucking at the curve between her neck and shoulder. Her back arched involuntarily, thrusting her ass against his bulging cock. She'd never wanted anybody this much in her entire life.

Black turned her in his arms, still gripping the back of her neck with one hand. His other came to rest lightly on her hip. He dipped down to nuzzle against her ear, each scrape of his rough stubble sending tendrils of desire quaking down into her belly.

She whimpered in response. Why were her legs going numb?

Black chuckled close to her ear, the rumble vibrating through his chest and into hers. Her hand was splayed between the perfect lines of his pecs, and the desire to feel his skin overwhelmed her. She lowered her palm and let her fingers slide beneath the hem of his shirt. He twitched, his breath leaving him in a hiss when her fingers made contact with his skin. His abs were like ripples of stone, his skin smooth and hot. She let her fingers play up over the ridges until she reached his chest, coming to settle right over his heart. The beat thudding beneath her palm threatened to melt her knees completely.

With a groan, he released her, stepping backward, his smoldering gaze locked with hers. "We need to get moving if we're going to make camp before dark. Go pack an overnight bag."

The break in contact made it feel like all the air had left the room. She leaned forward even as he backed away. Her palm tingled, remembering the beat of his heart. She could sense it was taking a lot for him to hold back. His obvious erection told her he was no more finished than she was, and yet he maintained his distance.

Renee cleared her throat. "Now who's the tease?"

He looked over his shoulder at her, features shadowed by the brim of his hat. "Oh, I promise I'm not teasing. But I'd prefer not to have an audience. We ride in five minutes."

Audience? She looked around the barn in confusion. There was no one in sight, not even Petunia, who'd retreated into her stall. Only a gorgeously blonde palomino stood watching them from the paddock outside. The horse flicked its tail, gaze disconcertingly intense, and Renee decided she might agree with Black in this instance. That horse was beautiful, but it gave her the creeps.

Breaking eye contact, Renee headed toward the house to gather her toothbrush.

*B*lack kept his gelding abreast of Renee and
Petunia wherever the trail would allow as
he guided them up the plateau. The sensation of Lori
watching him seduce Renee had set him on edge, and he
was working hard to leave the leader's scrutiny behind.

Ahead, the sun sat low on the horizon. They'd been
riding almost an hour, climbing a gradual rise toward one
of his favorite camping spots. Renee swung her head to
scan the dry landscape, orange sunlight illuminating the
tips of her hair with fire. "Where did my grandfather
die?"

The question caught him off guard. He'd been to the
spot many times since the accident, trying to picture
how his grandma could've fallen. The path was narrow,

but even with Toliman on her back, it wasn't dangerous, and there were plenty of wide spots to pause and rest. He sometimes wondered if she'd been running for some reason. To or from something, he'd probably never know for sure. Clearing his throat, he pointed to his left toward the canyon. He couldn't see the sharp drop, but he knew it was there. "Over there."

She reined back, bringing Petunia to a halt. "Who found him?"

"Lori." He stopped a few paces ahead. "The medical examiner determined he died on impact. No suffering." His voice sounded a scratch too high in his ears. There'd been no exam on Gloryanna. As the ranch vet, he could've done a post-mortem himself, but he couldn't bring himself to cut open his already mangled grandmother. And no one seemed concerned enough to ask.

"What was he doing there?" she asked.

"Someone said there was a yearling stranded over at Pearson's Point. He and my...Gloryanna went to help."

"Gloryanna?" Renee shaded her eyes against the low sun. "Someone else was with him?"

"His horse. She was special to him. A very special lady to all of us." Black's stomach felt sour talking about this. The herd had mourned the loss of the Lead Mare in their own way, assembling for a gallop from east to west across the plateau to follow the sun. He'd only been able to join them as a rider, not a runner. Remote as the ranch was, tourists still drove a rutted trail over the reserve's northern ridge to view the wild horses. Governmental wild-herd managers came to count heads and do roundups. Even airplanes flying over could notice the misshapen figure of a centaur. As a result, he was constrained to joining the herd at night, lingering on the outskirts of the family units while they slept, routing away any would-be predators.

Renee blessed him with a soft smile. "You're very much like my grandfather, I think. You love horses."

He adjusted his hat and looked out over the horizon. "They're my life."

"I wish I'd come back to see him." Her voice was high and light, like she was fighting back tears, and he regretted they were on horseback so he couldn't reach out and comfort her.

"He'd be glad you're here now, looking after his horses."

They stood a few minutes in silence, looking toward the canyon and allowing the horses to snatch mouthfuls of grass. The sun painted vibrant colors across the horizon, and the evening breeze carried a dusty, resinous scent only a hot day could leave behind. Renee nudged Petunia forward, and the tension left Black's shoulders. He hadn't realized how much the area still bothered him.

He directed the horses off trail, up a gradual incline that would lead them to a spot protected by ponderosas and a cluster of giant boulders he'd played around as a child. As if sensing the end of the journey, Petunia bumped up to a trot, jouncing Renee in the saddle. "How much longer until we reach camp? I think I'm getting saddle burn."

He laughed. "Regret not running away with your friend?"

"I've done some crazy stuff, but jumping off a building in a wing suit? No thanks."

"Not to mention the whole going to jail thing." His heart thudded a little harder at the thought of her in prison.

"Yeah, prison in Dubai doesn't sound like a good idea. Thanks for sticking up for me on that, by the way." She grinned at him.

"I'm a regular knight in shining armor." He tipped his hat, then pointed to several dark figures outlined against the horizon. His wild kin were less skittish than shifters. "Wild horses."

"Are they all wild out here?"

"Pretty much. Your land borders the Reserve. We can camp over there." He gestured with a nod toward a jumble of rocks not too far off where he'd spent the night many times before.

She guided Petunia that direction. "How much of this belongs to the ranch?"

"Around a hundred and eighty acres. Your granddad refused to fence it. He wanted it left open to the wild horses." *And the herd.* He was aching to tell her. To show her. But he was trapped here on this gelding instead of his own legs. His mind wandered to what it might feel like to have her legs clutched tightly against his centaur's withers, her breasts pressing into his bare shoulder blades as she held on from behind. His human body tingled with a desire to shift, and the gelding beneath him danced sideways as if sensing an imminent change.

"Whoa, there." He used the pressure of his knees to calm the creature and shoved the shifter magic down.

Petunia had continued without him, her head bobbing in time to her stride. She was an unimaginative beast, but that was a good thing for inexperienced riders. Like Renee and her glorious backside straddling the lucky horse. The boots sticking out of her capris looked ridiculous, but he wasn't going to tell her that after the struggle they'd had over wearing them. The curve of her bare shoulders and neck beckoned to him to kiss her there, nip her gently as a lover does. Pull her hips against him and make her moan as she rode his cock. He had an entire night with her under the stars ahead. Nudging the gelding, he caught up and passed her at a canter. Petunia knew the way from here.

Drawing up next to a ponderosa pine, he dismounted, tied his gelding to one of the branches, and began to unpack the saddle bags. The sky had turned lavender overhead, and beams of light poked through the dusty motes above the sagebrush. By the time Renee arrived, he'd thrown down a picnic blanket and popped open a bottle of wine.

He reached up to help her dismount, running a hand from her knee, up her thigh to her hip, ending with a cheeky pat against her bottom. "You've got a nice seat on a horse."

She grinned down at him. "You're the expert."

"Indeed I am." He kept his hand on the swell of her ass, maintaining eye contact like he never would with a herd member. He loved that he felt no need to look away, no need to play the ranking game. In fact, it felt like she was inviting him to take charge.

Renee made a face and swung her leg over the saddle. "I don't remember Cookies hurting my ass like this."

Her ass hovering at face level made his jeans feel tight, and he kept his hands on her hips a bit longer than necessary to help her down. She turned in his grasp, looking up at him with an impish smile. "Have any cowboy remedies for me?"

He brushed a strand of hair from her forehead, letting his fingertip trail around the curve of her ear and down the side of her neck. "'Fraid you're just going to have to ride this one out."

She trembled beneath his touch, closing her eyes and lifting her chin in invitation. Much as he wanted to kiss her right now, he knew better than to start down that path before setting up camp. He wanted to take his time with her, not be fumbling in the dark with a tent.

He brushed his lips across hers in a feather-light caress. "How about you scout for firewood while I finish setting up? Then we can talk some more about my cowboy remedies."

She opened her eyes, her pupils taking up most of her irises, lips in a playful pout. "Work, work, work."

He stepped back and allowed her to pass, swatting her butt cheek lightly. She squeaked and hop-skipped a step forward. "All right, all right. Firewood."

He gave himself the briefest moment to appreciate her swinging hips before tending to Petunia, thankful she was a normal horse instead of a shifter.

7

*R*enee held out the wine bottle to offer Black the last few drops. She'd been ready to pounce on him all night, but he seemed to want to take things slow. To savor her. The anticipation only made her hotter for him. Everything from a palm pressed to her lower back as she bent to spread out her bedding to the way he let his smoldering gaze linger on her in the dusky light made her panties dampen and heat creep up her thighs.

She held up the last triangle of goat cheese and arugula sandwich. "This is fancier than I imagined for a cowboy camping trip."

He surveyed the fire through the contents of his wine glass. "I roomed with a culinary student while I was at vet school. He was always bringing home weird leftovers, and I was a starving student. Guess I developed a taste."

"You went to vet school? So, are you a vet?" She'd thought him a simple creature, a one-note kind of flavor. But she was slowly discovering Black had many layers. Maybe that's why he was taking things so slow.

"You find that hard to believe?" He raised an eyebrow at her.

"No. I mean yes. I mean..." She licked her lips. "For some reason I never pictured a cowboy vet before. I thought vets were all doctory, with white coats and stethoscopes and stuff." She'd actually never met a vet, not that she could remember.

"I've used my share of stethoscopes. But it's kind of hard to keep that white coat clean when you're mucking out horse stalls."

She laughed. "But you grew up here on the ranch?"

"I was born in the city. My mom died when I was a baby and my grandmother brought me here. I've called it home ever since."

"Is your grandma still around?" So far she'd only met Black, Lori, and the housekeeper, Emile, but she knew there were about a dozen employees on the ranch, most of whom had worked for her grandfather for decades.

Black shook his head, looking down at his lap. "She died about the same time as your granddad."

Renee's heart twinged and she took a breath. Here she'd been playing up the pity card with a deceased grandfather and didn't even know Black's wound was just as fresh. Actually fresher, since his grandmother had actually been a part of his life. "I'm sorry. I didn't realize."

He looked up, a half smile lighting his features. "I remember you from when you were little, you know."

"You do?" She tried to dredge up his face in her memories. "Why don't I remember you?"

"I was a cocky teenager." He took a sip of wine and winked at her. "Too proud to talk to an eight-year-old girl who only wanted to chase barn kittens."

"Oh!" She laughed. "You can't be that much older than me!"

"Five or six years is a lot when you're that age. Not so much now." He set his wine aside on the blanket they shared. "I was sorry when your mom passed. She was good to me."

Renee felt tears prick her eyes. "It happened so fast. One minute she was helping me with homework, and the next I was sitting at a funeral. It was confusing. Dad called her cancer a curse."

"Cancer is an evil thing." His eyes were soft in the firelight.

She grit her teeth, remembering her dad's ranting against evil curses, searching for anyone, anything to blame for his wife's death. As a terrified little girl, she'd bought into the frenzy and fear. But later she began to wonder if the true evil wasn't Mom's death, but how Dad had let the loss affect him. "Do you believe in evil? I mean real evil?"

Black took a deep breath and lay back against the blankets, staring up at the stars. "Not to be trite, but there's a little bit of evil in all of us."

"Dad claimed the cancer was punishment for Grandfather's evil spells." She watched closely to see what Black thought of that bit of mysticism.

He snorted. "Your granddad didn't have an evil bone in his body."

She raised her brows at him. "I thought there was a little evil in all of us?"

He turned to look at her, throwing out one arm like an invitation.

Her insides quivered, the anticipation that had been bubbling through her all night shooting straight to the juncture of her thighs. Yet he'd taken things so slow, she didn't want to just dive right in. Not yet. She leaned forward on hands and knees and scooted toward him, stopping to stare down into his face.

He curled his hand around her knees on the blanket, like a half-circle of protection. His voice was soft as he said, "Well, if he had any, I never saw it. He was a good man. Can I tell you a secret?"

She nodded. She wanted to know every deep, dark thing this man held dear. To tighten the heartstrings that had wrapped themselves around her without her even realizing they were there.

"Your grandfather's treasure's part of this ranch. You can't separate the two."

Goosebumps pimpled her flesh. She whispered, "What is it?"

His hand tightened against her hip. "The horses here. The horses are the treasure."

She frowned. "I know Grandfather loved his horses, but how can they be a buried treasure?"

Black's eyes darkened and he dropped his hold. "I've said too much. More than I'm allowed."

"Allowed? Why are you not allowed?"

He turned his gaze from her face to the stars. "Go back to the will. Read it closely. Consider before you sell the ranch. That's all I can give you."

What the hell was going on around here? She and Black had gone from butting heads about footwear to molten lust to a connection she couldn't begin to explain in the course of a single evening. And now there was some sort of weird Nancy Drew secret going on. Was her father right about the black voodoo and midnight spells? "If there's something valuable here, why didn't he just tell me? Why leave a cryptic poem?"

"I can't say for sure. I only know he cherished each and every living being on this ranch. He wanted them taken care of. You should think about that before you make any decisions."

Her throat swelled, making it hard to speak. The longer she was here, the less she wanted to part with her inheritance. And with the cowboy who was part of it. In spite of Black holding back right now, Renee felt closer to him than she'd felt to any human being since the death of her mother.

"I can't afford it."

"The ranch won't cost you anything," he said earnestly. "We've always made do."

"That's great, but I need the cash." She gulped, thinking about how quickly the trust fund Mom had left her had disappeared.

"Are you in trouble?" His hand tightened on her leg.

"No," she said. "I'm just... out of money. These adventures with Steph cost a lot."

For a few heartbeats, he studied her, firelight wavering over his face. "Seems to me you might not actually like the adventures in the first place."

She flushed. He hardly knew her, yet he seemed to be able to read her soul. Lately the adventures had become burdensome. Renee thought more and more often of settling down in one spot. Selling the ranch would buy her a few more years, but then what?

He put a hand on her shoulder and guided her to lie beside him, pillowing her cheek in the hollow where his pec met his shoulder. Wrapping his arm behind her, he fitted her body against his and asked, "What do you do for a living, anyway?"

The question embarrassed her. At twenty-five years old, she'd never worked a day in her life. Mom's trust fund was supposed to have set her up as an adult; paid for school, bought a house, whatever. Instead, she'd squandered it on things like paragliding, swimming in shark cages, and chickening out of running with the bulls not once, but twice. "I'm between jobs."

"What do you *want* to do for a living?" His fingertips played delightful tickles up and down her spine, making it difficult to think.

"I like to cook." Not that her adventures with Steph left much time for cooking. "And I like to read." Not much time for that, either, come to think of it. "I used to really like riding horses."

He stiffened. "You didn't today?"

She traced her fingertips over the ridges of his chest. "Oh, I did. Although my backside might disagree."

Lowering his hand to cup her ass, he spoke into her hair. "You just need to re-train your muscles. I could help you."

The embers simmering in her core flamed to life once again. The heat seemed to burn away all her witty responses. "I'm sure."

He took a deep breath of her hair. "You smell delicious," he said, voice low and gravelly.

"Like what?" Her gaze was fixed on the growing lump in his jeans.

He rolled toward her, hoisting up on his elbow to stare down into her face. "Spring orchards and hot-blooded female."

Gulping, she lifted a hand to trace the stubbled line of his jaw. "That's quite a combination."

His free hand slid down her ribcage and over her hip, coming to rest over her sex. She inhaled sharply, her back arching against the hard ground. The heat of his hand through her capris made her flood her panties with moisture. He eased a fingertip between her thighs.

"I can smell when you want me."

"Like now?" she murmured mindlessly, lifting herself to meet the pressure of that finger.

Dipping his face to hers, he blotted out the starlight, capturing her lips. It wasn't a gentle or questioning kiss. It was demanding. Hard and focused. Chills raced across her skin as he thrust his tongue between her lips and claimed her. His fingers maintained pressure against her sex, and the weight of his body over her overwhelmed her senses. She wanted this, wanted him. No fooling around this time. She wanted every inch of him.

She fumbled at his waist for the tongue of his belt. God, she was bad at this. When was the last time she'd had sex, anyway? It didn't matter. She wanted this man, and she wanted him now.

He let out a soft, sexy noise deep in his throat and let her fumble a moment more before reaching down and flicking the belt loose. She yanked his zipper down and thrust her fingertips into the gap, locating the firm rounded head of his cock. He let out another soft groan, and nipped against her lower lip. His abs went rigid while he shoved his pants down his thighs.

He eased himself against her, and the hard length of his erection threatened to burn through the thin material of her capris. Cupping a hand behind her neck, he used the other hand to drag her waist hard against him. His tongue stroked her mouth rhythmically, spiraling the kiss into new heights of pleasure. He ran his hand up her ribs, dragging the thin material of her tank top with it. She raised her arms above her head so he could pull the garment free. He flung the flimsy material somewhere into the darkness and then was back on her, kissing her as he reached around to unsnap the clasp of her bra.

Cool night air hardened her nipples, followed by the hot wet heat of his mouth. Before she could exhale, he had the waistband of her capris undone and was peeling both them and her panties down her legs, her bare feet kicking the fabric free. She lay there naked in the firelight, him on his knees above her, as he stared down, drinking in her body with his eyes. His jeans hung part way down his thighs, allowing his massive erection free, but the rest of him was still covered, which seemed wrong on this glorious, sex-scented evening. Renee bolted upright, shoving his tee shirt up his torso. Her palms skimmed the hard ridges of his muscles before he reached down and grasped the hem, nearly ripping the material off his body before flinging it into the night to join her tank top and capris.

He grabbed her and flung her back to the blankets, one hand beneath her hips. She wrapped her legs around him, urging him closer. His mouth found hers again, sucking the breath from her with his impassioned kiss. He ground his hips, hitting her in exactly the right spot, his erection rolling against her slick folds and leaving her trembling.

His body was shaking now, too, a low noise rumbling deep in his throat. He grabbed her wrists in one hand and pushed them over her head, nipping kisses down her throat to the hollow of her neck and shoulder. God, was he a forceful, sexy man.

The dying embers of the fire cast shadows within shadows. Black lifted himself into a pushup above her, allowing her to view his incredible body, his incredible strength. Chest heaving with passion, deep ridges outlined every one of his muscles. His eyes seemed to have an almost feral glow. He dragged his hungry gaze from hers and traced his attention almost tangibly across her lips, down her throat, to the electrified peaks of her nipples. The head of his cock waited directly against her entrance, pressing only hard enough to tease her with his girth.

She let out an incomprehensible murmur, arching her back, trying to take him in.

With infuriating slowness he pushed into her, millimeter by millimeter, stretching her.

"Ride me," she whimpered, too trembly inside to scream. Then louder, "Hard!"

The sexy noise in his throat vibrated louder and he thrust downward, burying himself, crushing himself against her. She bucked against him, yearning for a second stroke.

He held the grind, his hand still holding both of hers trapped above her head. She wriggled beneath him, driving herself mad. When she sought his face, she found a smirk there. The naughty cowboy was teasing her, tormenting her. And she loved it. Loved being at his mercy.

"More," she said on a breath.

He pulled back only to dip into her shallowly again, another kind of tease, another kind of pleasure. "Tell me what you want."

"You. Please. All of you. Give me everything."

Black thrust forward, hard and deep, and she cried out in pleasure. Oh God, this was perfect. So right, and he was sliding in and out of her hard and fast. He pounded against her clit with excruciating skill, over and over, filling her with a tingling she hadn't experienced in so long.

He released her wrists and lowered himself against her, flesh to flesh, belly to belly. His hard muscles slipped against her skin, the friction adding yet another layer of sensation. Had sex ever felt like this? A desperate need to go farther, faster, deeper. To envelop every bit of him, not just his cock.

Something blossomed in her chest, radiating outward like a glowing wave. This was mystical. This was unique. Like every cell in her body had come alive at once, and every pump of his cock made the wave rise higher.

He spread her legs wider, thrusting into her, pounding her, and she was ready. The wave crested, and she had no control over what was happening. She cried out and grabbed the back of his hair, clutching on for dear life.

The deep-voiced vibration in his throat erupted into something primal and wild. The sound tightened her core around the orgasm ripping through her, sent her into an explosion of pleasure that nearly made her lose consciousness. Black buried his face against her neck, his teeth against her skin as he rammed her, rode her, every muscle coiled. Pulsing ripples sent a second wave of pleasure through her as he shot his warmth into her. He reared back and bucked one last time, filling her with pleasure bordering on pain as flooding heat emptied inside her.

He collapsed on top of her, weight mostly on his elbows as his cock throbbed in time with her own aftershocks. Resting his forehead against hers, he hugged her tightly. "What just happened?" he asked.

She could barely catch her breath. "You've never had an orgasm before?"

He pulled back only enough to look into her eyes. "You're saying it's like that for you every time?"

If her heated skin could have flushed any more, she would have. But he was right. Two people couldn't get any closer than they were right now, connected at the hips, him buried deep inside her. And yet it felt like they'd just shared more. It felt like their souls had met.

Black rolled to the side, bringing her with him. She cuddled into his warmth, surprised at how cool the night air felt against her skin. "I don't... I know I talk a big game, but I don't just jump into bed with anyone. What we just did, that was... I don't know what that was. That was special."

"It's not fair," he said, his heart beating too fast under her cheek.

"What isn't?"

He swallowed audibly. "Relationships."

Renee sat up, her heartbeat matching his. Was that what this was? Were they in a relationship? If she was honest, she felt more vulnerable now than she ever had in her life. Her playful flirting had turned into something deeper than she'd anticipated. She craved him for more than just sex. They'd connected on a level she'd never thought possible. His touch made her feel alive again. She wasn't merely someone else's shadow waiting for that someone to make the next move so she could follow. This man made her feel tall. Like he understood what it was like to need to fit in, no matter the cost, and he didn't expect her to act like someone else to make him like her.

She covered her breasts, suddenly self-conscious under his gaze, fighting the feeling deep inside her. *Get a grip, Renee. It's not like he said he loves you.* Yet how was she supposed to respond?

Before she could form the words, Black bolted upright. His attention seemed to be focused on the darkness outside camp, like he'd heard something.

"What is it?" she asked.

Then a woman's scream pierced the night.

8

---

*B*lack was on his feet in an instant, ears alert. He'd heard the horses shifting uncomfortably, but had ignored it. Now he wanted to kick himself for growing careless. For losing himself so completely in the mind-blowing sex. He bent to help Renee to her feet.

She rose, pressing herself against him, her sweet scent mingling with the night air. Her voice trembled. "Was that a woman?"

"Mountain lion." Giving her a reassuring squeeze, he let go and moved to stoke the fire back to life. "It won't come near the fire."

Renee scrambled to find her clothes, pulling her tank over her head. Black dug in their gear and pulled out the .45 he carried for protection. He'd only had to use it once before, to warn off a bear that had been coming too close to the barn. "I'd better bring the horses in."

As he reached for his jeans, terrified whinnies from the wild herd cut through the night. The distinctive high pitched cry of a foal set Black's limbs trembling. *No.* Shifter herd or wild brethren, it didn't matter, he had a driving need to protect, especially the young.

He thrust the gun toward Renee. "You know how to use a gun?"

She stared at the weapon as if it might bite her. "N-no."

Still holding the pistol, he spun toward the herd's cries. His centaur form was stretching the seams of his control, bucking to be released. He took Renee by one shoulder and turned her toward the blaze, thinking fleetingly about leaving the gun. *Better not.* A gun in inexperienced hands could be more dangerous than helpful. "You'll be safe here. Keep the flames high. I'll be back."

"Wait! You're going out there naked?"

The power of the shift vibrated uncontrollably inside him. He called over his shoulder, "I'll be fine!"

Bounding from the camp, he held the change at bay until he was clear of the firelight. He couldn't allow Renee to see, not only because Lori forbade it, but also because he wasn't ready to expose himself. She'd think he was a monster.

The wildcat screeched again, the echo tapering to nothing as it routed its prey. Black's shift seized his muscles and bones, splitting his legs and shifting his elongating spine backward. He paused only long enough to stabilize his new footing, then galloped across the moonlit sagebrush, hooves thundering against the dry ground. His blood burned with the need to protect. He let his ears guide him. The wildcat had gone silent. It'd made its mark.

Heading for the pocket of unnatural silence, Black galloped forward. The sky outlined several horses in starlight. Millie's familiar slumped back stood at the outer edge, bravely facing into the night. He'd assumed the nearby group was a herd of wild cousins. If he'd known it was shifters, he might not have so readily made camp nearby.

Millie nickered in his direction, calling for aid. He drew close, scanning the group. Millie's baby was nowhere in sight. "Where's Ivy-Jane?"

The mare nickered again, hopping her front hooves up and down anxiously. If it hadn't been more dangerous to be in human form, she'd likely have shifted back. But a naked human would be just as tasty to a mountain lion as a helpless foal. He forced thoughts of Renee, alone at the camp, from his mind. The fire would keep her safe. Right now he needed to find Ivy-Jane. How had the foal gotten separated from her mother?

He clutched the gun in his right hand, glad for the extra protection. His centaur blood commanded every nerve in his body, seeming to grant his senses extra power as he scanned the night.

A terrified squeal split the darkness from the direction of the camp. He must've passed Ivy-Jane on his way to the herd. Spinning, he leapt over a tall clump of sagebrush and barreled toward the cries, adding his own voice to the night in hope of driving the predator away. "Ivy-Jane!"

The foal's pitiful cries grew louder as he approached. A frantic rattle of branches to his right slowed his approach. In a pit of darkness next to the rocks, the tiny foal struggled within a mat of brush. Atop the nearest boulder, a pair of glowing cat eyes caught the moonlight, and Black could make out the hunched shoulders of a big cat against the midnight sky. He raised his gun, straining to aim in the darkness.

And then a pinprick of fire rounded the stone.

A single stick of firewood held high above her head, Renee crept past the lion without even seeing it. The lion shifted its gaze to the helpless woman, and Black's chest felt like it was about to explode. "Renee, watch out!"

She whirled, facing the rock, her face a mask of terror in the flickering light of her makeshift torch. A scream as fierce as the wildcat's echoed from her throat, and she shoved the torch upward toward the coiled beast.

The cat drew back, one paw poised as if to ward off the attack. Then it turned and sprang off the far side of the stone, disappearing into the night.

Black's protective instincts spurred him on. He reached Renee's side without thinking. "Are you all right? I told you to stay by the fire!"

She stumbled back a few steps, staring up at him. Her mouth was a perfect circle of shock as her gaze traveled across his chest and over his heaving flanks.

Heat flooded his skin as he realized what she saw. A monster. *Him* as a monster. Gritting his teeth, Black shoved his emotions down. There was no way to undo the damage. He'd deal with the repercussions later. Right now he had to keep both Renee and Ivy-Jane out of the mountain lion's jaws. He shoved the gun into Renee's hand. "Hold this." Plunging through the wiry branches ensnaring the foal, he snapped limbs and plowed through leaves. "It's okay, darling. I'm here. You're all right."

He reached the little horse and knelt to slip his arms beneath her belly, untwining her gangly legs from the grasping branches. Backing out of the mat of foliage, he was relieved to see Renee still waiting, her make-shift torch flickering down to a glowing red coal. He set Ivy-Jane on her feet, but the foal cried out and immediately collapsed.

Black felt sick to his stomach. "She may have a broken leg."

"What do we do?" Renee's voice cracked and wavered, and her eyes locked on the foal. At least she wasn't freaking out completely.

He needed to get everyone back to the fire before the mountain lion regained its courage, and the fastest way to do that was to carry them. He knelt to scoop the foal into his arms again and shot a sideways look at Renee. He'd never had a rider before, but how hard could it be? "Get on."

Even through the darkness, he could feel the weight of her shocked stare. "Wh-what?"

"That cat may return at any moment, and I have two easy meals in my charge. Now get on."

For a moment, she seemed undecided. Then she dropped her torch and ground it into the dirt, stabbing it deeply to ensure it was extinguished. Shifting the gun to her right hand, she used her left to steady herself against his shoulder and swung a leg over his back. As her weight settled against his spine, his hide shivered in a strange sort of pleasure. But he didn't have time to contemplate that now.

"Ready?" he asked.

He felt her nod, and lurched to his feet.

*R*enee clung to Black's shoulders and concentrated on the man in front of her rather than the horse beneath her. What the hell was he? She thought back to her semester of Greek mythology in high school. A satyr? No, she seemed to recall that was a goat-man. *Centaur.* That was it. She gripped her knees against his sides as he trotted back toward camp. The ride was less jarring than on Petunia, and she didn't know if that was because he made the effort for her, or if centaurs just naturally had a smoother gait.

Centaur. How could such a thing be possible? The thought flitted through her mind that perhaps he'd brought her out here camping and drugged the wine or something. She had to be experiencing a vivid hallucination. But his shoulder beneath her hand, not to mention his rippling flanks now between her legs felt very real.

And there was another thought. Between her legs. She'd just had sex with this man, this creature. A man with a stallion for an alter ego. And how could he be a man one minute and a centaur the next?

They reached the camp and Black lay the foal down next to the fire. The poor little thing curled up in a heap and closed her eyes, obviously exhausted. Once again Black knelt, his head drooping as he waited for Renee to dismount. She slid free, breaking contact reluctantly, despite her confusion.

Black's not human. The concept made her legs weak. But the magnificent creature kneeling before her was real.

She didn't understand any of this. But she liked Black. He was sexy and protective and… really good in bed. At a complete loss on how to address anything that had just happened, Renee said, "Well, tonight was… exciting."

Chest heaving from the effort of carrying both her and the foal, he gritted, "Why didn't you stay put like I asked you?"

"Our horses got loose." She pointed into the darkness, heart racing as she recalled the thundering hoofbeats coming out of the darkness. "They ran right through our camp and almost on top of me. And then I heard what turns out to be Ivy-Jane crying for help. You said the mountain lion didn't like fire, so I thought maybe I could scare it off and save what sounded like a baby."

He lurched to his feet, hooves striking the dirt with purposeful intensity as he turned to face her. "You could have gotten yourself killed."

She threw back her shoulders, her blood boiling. How dare he be angry at *her*? "I was worried for you. You ran out there all alone! How was I supposed to know you had a secret superpower?"

He stopped his advance, mouth twitching as if fighting back a smile. "Secret superpower?"

She flung out a hand to gesture at his sleek legs. "What do you call it? I didn't even know there was such a thing as a centaur-horse-shapeshifter whatever you're called. I've heard of werewolves, but a were-horse? Is that what you are?"

His eyes danced with amusement, and his mouth looked a little less glum. "Not exactly. But there are horse shapeshifters. And I wasn't supposed to tell you."

"Well, you didn't exactly tell me, did you?" She made a sweeping gesture, telling him to look at himself.

Black broke into a resigned laugh.

Her irritation ebbed a fraction. He was sexy when he laughed. "Are there more of you?"

He pressed his lips together and looked away.

He said he couldn't talk about it. She wondered why, but didn't prod him again. What did she know of the magic or whatever it was that allowed him to do this, to be this mythical creature? Maybe he'd turn into a pile of ash if he talked about it. Her gaze shot to the exhausted foal. "Is she going to be okay?"

"I don't know." He shifted his weight uncomfortably.

"Well aren't you a vet or something? Can't you tell?"

"I need to examine her more closely, but it's difficult in this form."

She frowned, confused. "Can't you change back?"

"I... can. I just... I don't shift in front of people. Not even my herd."

"Oh." For some reason that statement hurt. They'd just made the most impassioned, intense love she'd ever experienced in her life, and now he didn't want to show her this part of himself? "I can turn my back."

She spun, crossing her arms and staring into the darkness, her heart shriveling a little at the way he shut her out. She shouldn't care. It was only sex, right? But she'd believed Black was letting her in, and in accepting that from him, she'd become vulnerable herself. Her head told her to let it go, but her heart wanted to cling to him, like she'd found a perfect mate in a man of a different ... species? Was this even okay? He wasn't human. Could something like this even work? Her vagina certainly seemed to think so. Stupid vagina.

A warm hand captured her shoulder and tugged her around to face him. He was still a four-legged fiend, towering over her with that sexy, sweaty chest all glistening in the firelight. She licked her lips, her own chest tight with anxious thoughts. "I thought you were going to change—shift—whatever you call it?"

Ribbons of dust and electricity surrounded her, stinging her eyes and prickling against her skin like lightning about to strike. She threw up a hand to shield herself. Through her teary vision, the shadow against the fire shrank from massive equine height to Black's only slightly-less-massive human height. She rubbed her eyes with the backs of her wrists and found herself looking at a butt-naked Black, standing square before her, his eyes glittering in the firelight.

The hardened shell she'd been building around her heart crumbled. He'd let her in after all. Shown her what he claimed he showed no one, not even his own kind. She wanted to laugh. She wanted to cry. She wanted to pound her fists against him with helpless abandon. Helpless because she'd never felt so close, so vulnerable to anyone in her life.

Black turned away, his attention now on the injured foal. She let her gaze linger on his naked back. Caring for the helpless foal, he looked so sure, so powerful and confident, so beautiful all at once. She could almost convince herself the centaur had been a hallucination. How could it possibly be real? The only explanation was magic, and she'd never believed in magic. In fact, she'd rejected it, leaving it to her father's ranting.

Everything she knew about the world had just crashed into itself, leaving her reeling and confused.

Renee moved toward the flames, thinking at least she might be able to lend a hand with the foal. The sound of hooves in the darkness once again drew her up short. The pounding stopped, and two shadowy figures emerged into the flickering firelight, a slightly older man with deep-set midnight eyes and tattoos down both arms, and Lori, her blonde hair mussed as if she'd just been on a joyride in a convertible. Both were stark naked.

Renee's gaze flicked between Black and the newcomers. Did this mean Lori was a centaur-shifter, too? How many of them were there?

Black rose to face Lori. "I didn't tell her."

The blonde smiled and shook her head, holding her hands up palm out as if to settle him. "Of course not, Black. But the cat's out of the bag now, isn't it?"

He edged toward Renee, placing himself between her and the visitors. "Her granddad knew and kept our secret. Give her a chance."

Renee shook her head. "Grandfather knew? Is everybody on the ranch a centaur?"

Lori let out a low chuckle, her too-perky breasts bobbing with the sound. "Of course not, honey. Only Black here is burdened with that deformity. The rest of us are purebreds through and through."

"Deformity?" Renee's mind swam. "He looked rather magnificent to me."

"Never mind, Renee." Black kept his eyes on Lori and the other man. "We can talk about all that later. Ivy-Jane's hurt. I need to carry her back to the ranch where I can take care of her."

"Then go. Survival of the fittest, they say." Lori's gaze wasn't on Black or the foal. It was on Renee.

Ice crept up Renee's spine.

The strange man stepped gracefully into the circle of firelight. Something about him reminded her of Black. The light caught his eyes with a reflective glow that reinforced these people weren't human. His voice was gruff, nostrils flaring. "I'll carry the human for you, Black."

Behind him, a look of annoyance crossed Lori's gaze. Then her smirk returned. "I knew I'd make a mount out of you, Saul. Go on, then."

Black's jaw muscles visibly bunched in the firelight, and Renee flushed, remembering Lori's offer to saddle a stallion this afternoon. "This is Saul? The stallion you didn't want me to ride?"

Casting an apologetic glance her way, Black said, "Saul's my uncle. He'll take care of you."

Renee raised her brows. "You didn't seem to think so earlier."

"It's different now," Black said.

"How?"

Saul crossed his arms, orange flickers glinting off hard lines of muscles. The guy was built like a brick house. "Well, you smell like sex, for one. Sex with my nephew. I'm not going to touch that."

Horror filled Renee's mind. First of all that she stank like sex. Second, that there seemed to be some sort of unspoken agenda among these horse people. Why had Lori offered to saddle Saul for her earlier? "Do I get a say in all this?"

Lori pursed her lips in a coy sort of tease. "Unless you want to stay behind and face the lion on your own, honey, I suggest you ride whichever stallion is willing to get between your legs.

Renee's heart threatened to jump from her chest it was beating so hard. Lori put her nerves on edge. But then, riding a strange stallion shifter didn't sound much better. What should she do? Their mounts had run away, and she had no idea how to get back on her own, let alone in the dark. "Can Ivy-Jane wait until morning?"

Black shook his head. "She needs medical attention."

A glance at the foal told Renee it was true. The baby horse's dun-colored flanks were shivering in spite of the warm night and the heat from the fire. Renee took a deep breath. "All right, Saul. Show me what you've got."

*a*fter setting Renee down just outside the barn, the shifters had almost seemed to forget about her as they hurried to tend the foal. She'd slipped away to her room to find some time to think, away from mountain lion screams, thundering hooves, and magical creatures beyond any girl's wildest dreams for a pony. Now in the early morning light, Renee stumbled out of the house with a travel-mug of coffee in one hand and her phone in the other. Her inner thighs ached from the unaccustomed riding yesterday—both kinds. The yard was quiet this morning, the tension from the previous night dampened by the dewy air.

Gravel crunching loud beneath her borrowed boots, she approached the barn. A quaking desire to see Black twisted her stomach, and not just to have her questions answered. She was afraid of him, but not for the reasons others might think. Centaurs and shape shifters? Those were cool. Her fear went deeper. Black had touched something inside her. He didn't play games like the men she met with Steph, and he seemed to understand what losing her grandfather meant to her. She'd even flirted with the idea what they had was something unique. Love was one thrill she'd avoided with a passion, and yet here she was, facing a fall if she took a single step forward.

But Black was a mythical creature. Did he even think like a human? She'd tried to Google information on centaurs and shape shifters, but cell service was spotty at the ranch and she couldn't get many web pages to load. Grandfather apparently hadn't owned a computer, let alone wi-fi.

Black seemed to think he was some sort of deformed monster. All Renee could see was a man with a superpower he used to protect her and a baby horse from an awful predator. The connection they'd shared last night lingered in her blood like a drug. Her inner thighs tingled with memory, the bones down there aching from more than the extended horseback ride. *I want to ride a cowboy...*

She froze in front of the open bay door, steam from her coffee hitting her face like a wake up call. She obviously needed some space or else she might just let her hormones forget all the craziness from last night. If she went to town, she could find a coffee shop with wi-fi and do a little research. Think this through before she got any deeper.

Turning, she stared at the empty gravel parking area between the house and the barn. Steph had taken the rental when she'd left. Renee hadn't worried then, figuring Black or someone could get her to Missoula to catch a flight home. Now she was stranded here alone, surrounded by who-knew how many shapeshifters, with no transportation of her own.

Her gaze drifted to a smaller building she remembered as a machine shed from her younger days. Grandfather kept a tractor in there for hauling hay and raking pasture. *You going to drive a tractor to town?* She smirked at the idea. But maybe he had a car or something in there to haul supplies from town.

She shoved against the side door to get it open and entered. The dark building smelled of stale oil, metal filings, and dust. She left the door ajar to let in light and moved past an ancient John Deere tractor and a well-ordered workbench. In the far bay sat a beat-up Chevy pickup with the keys in the ignition. *Score.*

Setting her coffee on the hood, Renee wrestled with the garage door, realized it was latched, and finally got it open. Morning air rushed in like the building had been holding its breath. She took a deep taste, savoring the sunlight painting the far-away tops of trees and the faint singing of birds. In spite of the excitement from last night, this place felt peaceful. Protected. Special. She could see making a home here. Maybe with Black.

"You're up early." Lori's voice startled her from the barn's side door. Her bling was back in place, right down to the Montana belt buckle covering most of her flat stomach.

The icy shiver Renee'd felt last night returned to the base of her spine. "So are you."

Lori sauntered over, coming to rest at the open garage door and leaning one shoulder against the frame. She crossed one boot over the other, thumbs hooked into her belt. Her gaze reminded Renee of a housecat watching a bird. *That makes me the bird...*

After a heartbeat of uncomfortable silence, Renee asked, "How's Ivy-Jane?"

Lori waved a manicured hand. "Black has it under control. He has the touch. But then, you already know that."

Heat flooded Renee's face, and she turned to retrieve her coffee mug. Sex with Black had been mind-blowing, satisfying in a way she'd never expected or experienced before, and a big part of her resented that others seemed to want to belittle it—first Saul, and now Lori. She decided to play innocent. "He seems like a really good vet."

As if she hadn't heard, Lori continued. "Women like you come and go. But Black's special. I can't have you breaking his heart."

Renee's desire to play nice burned away like a flash of gunpowder. She spun, her chest tight. What right did this woman have to judge her? "I didn't exactly get the impression you liked Black all that much."

Lori shrugged. "I have a duty to protect my herd. Whether I like them or not."

"Well, I *do* happen to like him, so you can just bugger off and mind your own business." Renee's blood boiled. Partly because Lori rubbed her the wrong way, and partly because she didn't want to face that she really did like Black. A lot.

Lori's hands rose in front of her, palm out. "No need to attack me. I'm only looking out for my own. Your grandfather understood."

Renee's urge to jump in the Chevy and drive right over this bitch warred with her need to have answers. "If Grandfather knew about shifters, why didn't he tell me?"

"The herd's only refuge is this ranch, and your grandfather used our dependence to his advantage. How do you think he kept this place running without paying a dime in wages? Though I have to give him credit for keeping his promise to Gloryanna."

Frowning, Renee looked out over the empty parking area and silent morning pastures as if she might find the answer there. She hadn't considered how everything had continued running in the time since her grandfather's death. Finances had never been her thing. "What are you saying? That you're slaves?"

A smirk twisted Lori's face. "What do you call a worker who doesn't get paid?"

Renee grit her teeth, refusing to take Lori's bait. "Volunteers. No one's forcing you to stick around."

"Ah, there she is. Old Toliman's granddaughter." Lori's lip curled. "Deluding yourself that keeping the herd's secret justifies the exploitation of its members."

"I never said that." Renee clenched her hands into fists at her sides.

Lori's face sobered. "Then prove it. Join us."

"How?"

"Marry Black."

Taking a step back, Renee shook her head, unsure she'd just heard correctly. Marriage? In what kind of fantasy world was this woman living? But then, in what kind of fantasy world were centaurs and shapeshifters real? Black was something other than human, something more. Who knew what the rules were in this crazy version of reality? And she *had* been fantasizing about making a home on the ranch with him. "We just met two days ago."

"Time's meaningless." Lori arched an eyebrow. "Prove you consider us equal."

"I don't have to marry someone to consider them equal."

Lori smiled. "Look, I know you like Black. And he obviously likes you. The truth is, he'll never really be part of this herd, in spite of being Gloryanna's grandson. I'm trying to look out for him."

Renee frowned, not appreciating Lori's subtext. "Why? Because he's different? What I'm hearing is that *you* don't consider *him* equal."

Confusion brushed across Lori's face, but she recovered with a look of pity. "I respect his dedication to the herd. It's just that the herd's very particular about bloodlines. There are so few of us left, we have to be choosy about our breeding partners."

"First of all, I'm not a *breeding partner*." Renee advanced on the tall woman, even though she had to look up into her face. "And second of all, there's nothing at all wrong with Black. He's perfect just the way he is, and you're a fool if you can't recognize that. Now if you'll excuse me, I'm going to check on Ivy-Jane."

Brushing past the woman, Renee stomped out of the garage, all thoughts of leaving the ranch gone.

10

*B*lack bolted awake to the slam of the barn's side door. Small, angry footsteps made a beeline for Ivy-Jane's hospital area. He sat on a straw bale just outside the open stall door with his back propped against the wall, eyes closed. He'd been unable to keep Renee out of his mind, even as he'd tended Ivy-Jane and withstood Lori's recriminations for revealing himself.

Renee's cherry-blossom scent filled the air, and the footsteps silenced. He could feel her energy while she stood there watching him. Was she frightened of him? He didn't blame her. Yet he didn't smell fear as the silence stretched longer and longer. He smelled the rich scent of arousal. He let her continue to look a good sixty seconds before drawling, "Morning, sunshine."

She released a startled squeak, then whispered, "Is that some sort of shifter sixth sense, knowing when someone's watching you?"

He sat up, a bleary smirk on his lips. Millie and the foal were asleep just inside the stall, so he kept his voice low as he rose. "You weren't exactly treading lightly when you came in here."

"Oh. Yeah." Renee cleared her throat and shifted her gaze toward the open door. Her face was flushed, and her shoulders heaved as if she'd been running. "How's the little one?"

He dusted hay from his jeans while he stepped away from the stall. He still wasn't wearing a shirt, but what he felt most naked without was his hat, which was still at the camp site. "Her leg's only sprained. She'll be up and around in a day or two." He plucked a tickling thread of hay out of the hair at the nape of his neck. "I'm more worried about her mental trauma."

"I can relate." Renee bit her lip.

Black felt himself frown, and tried to smooth his face without much success. There was so much to say now that the secret was out. But he didn't know where to begin. "This isn't the way I wanted you to find out."

Renee shook her head. "I still don't understand why Grandfather couldn't tell me."

Black glanced behind him toward Millie. She lay beneath a chevron blanket in human form next to Ivy-Jane, one hand resting on the foal's shoulder, her long, dull gray braid lying limp on the hay behind her. Her chest moved in the steady rhythm of sleep, but he wouldn't be surprised if she was listening. Lori hadn't lifted the ban on talking about the herd, but Renee already knew so much. *Enough to be dangerous,* as Lori had put it last night. Well, there was no going back. The secret was out. The only direction now was forward, right? With or without Lori's approval. Besides, this secret was Black's as much as hers. More so, maybe, because he had even more to hide.

Moving forward, he took Renee's arm and led her from the stall toward the pyramid of bales at the end of the barn. The loose straw on the floor prickled his bare feet. He headed toward an alcove where he sometimes retreated to satiate his un-herd-like desire for privacy. "Ask me whatever you want."

She glanced around, but didn't resist his guiding hand. He sat on a platform of bales he'd covered with a horse blanket, pulling her gently down next to him and trying to hide his disappointment when she chose to keep several hand-widths of space between them.

She twisted her fingers in her lap, her gaze on him guarded. "Lori wants me to prove I don't mean you harm."

His eye twitched. Of course Lori'd been on the prowl to catch Renee before he could this morning. Who knew what kind of lies that witch had already fed Renee about the herd? "Stay away from her, all right?"

"Why?"

"She bites. For real. Please, just stay away."

To his relief, Renee nodded. "All right, I'll try. But she's an in-your-face kind of person, isn't she?"

That made him chuckle. "That's one way to put it."

"She said you're Gloryanna's grandson. Wasn't that the last herd leader?"

He nodded.

"So, I take it she hates you because you're, like, a prince or something? A threat to her leadership?"

"A prince? No, we don't have royalty. I'm just a half-breed stallion. And besides, the Lead Mare's chosen by vote."

Her nose wrinkled in an adorable frown. "And they chose Lori? Why?"

"The herd respects Lori's knowledge of the outside world." His carefully phrased answer was the produce of a lifetime of ingrained respect for rank, but left a bitter taste in his mouth.

Renee rolled her eyes. "I don't think she knows as much as you give her credit for."

"Lori was captured as a foal and broken to ride like other domestic horses, which is humiliating for a shifter. When her first shift came over her, she escaped and lived on the streets until she found us. She spent years hiding among humans, hiding her shifter nature, learning about their ways."

"She didn't know how to get back to her family? How sad."

"The way she tells it, you wouldn't feel pity. She's tough —tougher than most equines—and not afraid to stand up for what she wants." Or to force her will on others, he thought. "The herd was in chaos after Grandma died. Lori stepped in and took over and no one ever complained."

"So if Lori's not worried about you taking over her leadership, why's she treat you so badly?"

Black shrugged. "The herd always tolerated me for Grandma's sake. But I'm different. Deformed."

"You're not deformed." She pulled herself back to look at him, one eyebrow raised. "I've heard of centaurs in Greek mythology. I've never heard of horse shape shifters. They're the deformed ones. Besides, aren't you all the same in human form?"

He smiled, appreciating her spunk. "Yes, but horse form is how we determine rank. While the rest of the herd can exist together day and night, horse and human, I can't because an outsider might see me. I never get a chance to fight for rank."

"But you could rank as a human. You're even a vet. That has to give you as much street cred as Lori. How come they didn't choose you?"

He shook his head. "Besides being a centaur, I'm male. Stallions can't lead the herd, not like the Lead Mare does."

"Why not?"

"Biology, I guess." Sighing, he tried to formulate how to describe herd hierarchy. "Herd society is sort of like a game of chess. The queen is the most powerful piece. The Herd Stallion—the king piece—has limited power."

Renee looked at her hands a few heartbeats before she met his gaze again. "You said you're a half-breed. Does that mean you're half human?"

He should have known she'd ask, but for some reason he wasn't ready. Most of the time there were hidden barbs when someone brought up his heritage, and he found it difficult to rein in his knee-jerk response to her perfectly innocent question.

"I'm sorry." She scooted closer and leaned her cheek against his biceps. "That was rude. I shouldn't have asked."

The contact dissipated his instinctive shield, replacing it with a surge of feeling in his chest he couldn't define, but that made him want to nuzzle against her neck and breathe deeply of her essence, preferably with his cock embedded in her wet heat. He settled for putting one arm around her, pulling her close to his bare chest. "Don't be sorry. It's a perfectly honest question. And I want to tell you." He put his chin atop her head and rested there a moment. "I'm... I need to start at the beginning. With my mother. Grandma said my mom wanted more than a podunk ranch could give her. She wanted to go back to the herd's nomadic roots. So she left. The herd hadn't been here at the ranch very long at that point, but that's a different story."

Renee readjusted her position, turning her cheek so she could gaze up into his face while he spoke. One hand slid up to rest palm-down over his heart. The contact of her smooth skin may as well have been a lasso around his soul.

He covered her hand with his free one, wrapping his fingers around hers, and continued talking. "My mom kept in touch, sent postcards from cities across the country, even made it to Alaska. The letters stopped suddenly without reason. Your grandfather helped search, I guess, hired an investigator to track her down. No luck. My mother had disappeared. Then, a couple of years later, a hospital in Chicago called with bad news. Or as Grandma liked to say, miraculous news." His chest ached with the memory of his grandma's voice in his ear while he sat on her lap as a child, and he clutched Renee's hand all the tighter against him. "Mom had given birth to a healthy baby boy. She'd told doctors the name of the ranch on her dying breath."

"Oh, Black!" Renee pulled her hand free and wrapped both arms around his waist, squeezing.

"That was the one and only time Grandma ever left the ranch. To retrieve me." He cleared his throat. "But to bring this story back to your question—we have no record of who my father is. The logical assumption is that I'm half-human."

Renee's shoulders rose and fell in a deep breath, her voracious hug remaining firmly in place around his waist. "I can say from personal experience that there's nothing wrong with you being human." Her breath was hot against his chest. "You're sexy as hell."

A laugh crawled up his chest and rolled from his mouth in an unexpected release. How could she make him feel whole in so few words? "Sexy, huh?"

Renee eased up on the embrace, fingers tickling over his bare skin, and murmured against his chest. "Incredibly."

"You're not put off by my centaur?"

She pushed him back against the blanket. "Mmm. That only makes you more sexy. I like to ride."

The rough blanket sank into the straw beneath his shoulder blades. He reached around and stroked the small of her back, letting his fingers slip into the gap between her shirt and her jeans. Her heart-shaped face had an impish grin while her palm skimmed his stomach, downward to his fly. His cock leapt to life at her touch, the scent of her arousal mingling with the smell of clean straw. He curled his fingers around the back of her neck and pulled her down into a kiss. Her mouth opened to him, and he rolled his tongue in a twining dance with hers.

Her hand over his fly cupped and massaged his balls while her mouth fired his blood. He reached around behind her and grabbed her jeans-covered ass, fingers dipping into the hollow between her legs as he palmed her backside. She moaned and clenched her butt, grinding her hips against him. His cock surged again in response. He growled, wanting to be in control. In one easy sweep he lifted her off him and rolled to bring himself on top, resting on his elbows above her. He didn't give her a chance to complain, but claimed her mouth again, crushing his lips against hers and plunging his tongue within her, tasting her sweet breath with every inhale.

He wanted to feel her skin, to explore every inch of her exquisite body. He thrust one hand beneath the hem of her shirt. Her skin glided like satin beneath his rough palm until he reached her bra and cupped the padding there. That had to go. He expertly slid his hand around her back and flicked the undergarment open, retracing his trail underneath the elastic to her waiting breast. Her nipple was hard and waiting for him. Kneading the soft flesh, he rolled the bud between his fingers.

With tiny, panting breaths, she fumbled at his waistline, trying to unfasten the button. "No," he said against her lips, catching her hand with his free one and pinning it to the blanket. He wanted to make her come with his hands and mouth alone. He wanted to make her yield to him and beg for him before he mounted her. He wanted to really believe she wanted him.

He caught her other wrist and brought both her hands above her head. Her wrists were so tiny and delicate, he could hold both in one hand. Keeping her trapped, he used his free hand to trace a teasing line across her lips and down her chin and neck to settle between her breasts over her heart. She arched her back, her ribs heaving with passion.

"You are so sexy," he whispered.

She licked her lips, and he wondered what it would be like to fuck that mouth. *Whoa, boy.* Right now this was all about her. He dropped his trailing finger beneath the partially-raised edge of her shirt and eased both it and her bra up, exposing her breasts. Her pert nipples jutted toward the rafters like a pair of spurs urging him onward. He dipped his head to one, tongue flicking out to sample the very tip. She whimpered, and he relented, taking the nipple into his mouth to tug and suck it into a tight peak. Then he nipped his way across her chest to give the other equal treatment.

She squirmed beneath him, but he held her hands firmly above her head. While he paid homage to her second nipple, he ran his palm over her belly to her sex, cupping the warmth there. Wet heat had soaked through her jeans, and he massaged her with the flat of his hand. She lifted her hips to grind against him, and he increased his speed until he sensed she was ready for the next level. Flicking open the top button, he slid his hand down the front and over her curls. His middle finger found her slit wet and ready, her clit throbbing beneath the pressure of his touch.

Sliding his finger in and out along the slit, he teased more moisture from her, plunging deeper with each stroke until his finger curled and found her opening. Her tight ridges clamped around his finger as he dipped inside.

She struggled against his grasp, her hips bucking in time to his thrusting fingers, searching for more. He continued to tease her opening, sliding over her clit with each stroke. Wetness soaked his hand. She wriggled beneath him, gasping for breath, words nearly incoherent. "I need more. Please."

He decided to oblige, freeing her hands so he could shimmy the fabric off her legs. Her scent filled the air with the heady flavor of her arousal and he sucked air into his mouth and over his palate, absorbing every juicy nuance. She groped for the buttons on his jeans. He cupped her face and kissed her deeply while she fumbled, each butterfly brush of her hands against his fly nearly sending him over the edge. The release of the buttons eased the pressure his cock had been exerting against his fly, and he had to remind himself to please her first. He grabbed her hands before she could expose him. "Not yet."

Getting to his knees, he reared back to look at her, drinking her in. Her flushed skin and gentle curves made him want to bite her, to nip her flanks and rub his face against her before he covered her with his body. He placed his hands on her breasts, kneading gently before sliding lower to mold against her ribs, thumbs tracing down her center line toward her belly button. There, he paused to circle her navel before continuing downward, thumbs leading the way into her curls. She gasped, hips flexing upward to meet him and her small hands flew to his wrists, urging him downward. Inward. He lifted his eyes to meet hers, the light of her passion burning bright as their gazes connected.

He slid along her lower lips, easing them open, spreading her legs with his palms at the same time. She blossomed like a flower, and he lowered his face to her folds. Her flesh quivered. He sucked gently, pressing his lips against her and probing his tongue into her heat while he continued the massage of her outer lips. Her fingers wove through his hair and she let out a moan that made his blood sizzle. He plunged his tongue hard into her opening once, twice, three times. She cried out, bucking upward against him, and her heated flesh pulsed and contracted with her orgasm, flooding his tongue with her juices.

He drank her up until he was sure she was finished, then he reared back up on his knees. Her chest heaved, hands fluttering weakly against the blanket. His cock could wait no longer. Shoving his jeans down around his hips, he freed himself and lifted her hips up and onto his waiting shaft. Again she cried out, calling his name, and he thrust into her, her circles of heat tightening around him in ecstatic embrace. With blinding fury, his release overtook him, and he buried himself inside her, pulsing into her core.

Shuddering, he dropped to his elbow over her and whispered, "I think I love you."

"I think I love you, too." She murmured.

11

*R*enee clutched weakly at Black's shoulders. Had she really just reciprocated the "L" word? Her blood pounded in her ears. It had to be hormones making her stupid. She couldn't be in love. Love was dangerous. To be avoided at all costs. Especially since she hardly knew the guy. Right?

Yet she knew more about him than she'd ever imagined possible.

Love for Black somehow felt empowering. Like acknowledging it would not just free her, it would make her whole. Complete her. And she hadn't even known she was in pieces. Well, some part of her had. Why else had she been drifting around after Steph, searching for that ever-elusive thrill that would somehow give meaning to her life?

She opened her mouth against his skin, circling her tongue to taste his earthy scent, scraping her teeth lightly across his flesh. He shuddered and turned his face to nuzzle against her ear, his breath hot. Black was amazing. Heart-throbbingly, knee-meltingly, amazing. Worthy of love.

No. No! She placed her palms flat against his chest, trying to push him away.

He rose only far enough to look down into her eyes. "Am I too heavy?"

"I need to get out of here." And yet everything important suddenly felt like it was right here, right now, and the thought of leaving made her want to plant her feet and stay.

Black rolled off her with graceful ease and rose to his feet. The air felt suddenly cold, and she jerked her shirt down over her torso. The small effort seemed to sap her willpower. The beautiful man back-lit by dusky light mesmerized her. She wanted to burrow into his arms. To wrap herself around him and never let him go.

What if she gave the relationship a go? She risked herself all the time at these stunts Steph arranged. Why not choose a stunt of her own? She might actually be good at this one. Might actually be able to have a white-picket-fence kind of life on the ranch, married to a real-life cowboy stud. She rolled over and reached for her pants. "Did you know Lori asked me to marry you?"

"No." He focused unwarranted intensity on fastening the buttons of his fly. "What'd you tell her?" His arms and chest flexed in sexy ripples of muscle. How could anyone think him anything but perfect?

She thrust her legs into her pants. "That what happens between you and I is our business. She can just get over herself."

He jerked his gaze to her, teeth flashing in a grin. "You'd make a fantastic Lead Mare."

She scowled and awkwardly scooted off the makeshift bench, looking for her shoes. "Yeah, no. Your herd is not my circus or my monkeys. Why they follow a narcissistic bitch like Lori is beyond me. How does marriage even work in the herd, anyway?"

Black held out a hand and pulled her to her feet. "There's a lot of dating around, I guess you'd say. Finding a life-mate is rare."

That answer made her chest feel like it had been stepped on. He'd said he loved her, but that apparently didn't have the same meaning for him as it did for her. Renee felt sick to her stomach. Blinking to keep her burning eyes from spilling tears, she elbowed past him. She would not let him see her cry. No, no, no. She'd wanted to ride a cowboy, and that's what she'd done. End of story.

Striding purposefully toward the door, she spoke without looking behind her. "I'm running to town. Text me if you need anything."

"Renee, wait. Is something wrong?"

She walked faster, pleased he was forced to mince across the sharp gravel driveway in his bare feet. Stupid Black. Making her love him when she'd been completely honest at the start that she wasn't interested in love. She reached the beat up Chevy and jerked the door open. The engine complained when she turned the key, but chugged to an uneven start, rattling her forgotten coffee cup off the hood.

He reached the garage and stood blocking her way. "Renee!"

Unable to hear him over the engine, she revved it louder, hoping the growl told him to get out of the way.

He moved toward the driver's side door and she threw the pickup into gear.

Nothing happened.

Black reached the window, making a rolling motion with one hand. Reluctantly, she rolled down the window. He leaned against the frame. "The transmission went out on this a while back."

Well, hell. She thumped the wheel with both hands in frustration, then turned the engine off.

Black remained leaning on the window frame. "Mind telling me what's wrong?"

The burning in her eyes was worse, tears clouding her vision. But she couldn't escape unless she slid across the bench seat to the other door.

As if sensing her thought, he looked down and took a step back. Her flight instinct eased a fraction. Taking a breath, she stared at him, this beautiful man who she wanted to punch in the face. Her heart hurt way more than it should. She'd only known him one day, and he was way out of her league. She should have let Steph have him.

"Renee, I don't know what I said or did wrong back there, but I wish you'd tell me."

"I'm not your wife or your life-mate or whatever. I don't have to tell you anything."

An infuriating smile curved his lips. "You're cute when you're jealous."

"I'm not jealous. I'm just... I don't sleep around. You... what we did was kind of special to me. Even if it wasn't to you."

Black's eyes glittered and he leaned forward, close enough for her to smell his hay and leather scent. "It was —is—special to me. I said life-mates were rare. Not impossible. And when a bond does happen, there is no going back."

Renee swallowed, lost in the depths of his gaze. It was like an electric field bound them together as they stared at each other. She wanted to love him more than anything in the world at that moment in time. "What are you saying?"

"I'm saying I've never shared myself with anyone like I've shared myself with you. When you saw me in my centaur form, I was terrified, but now I'm glad you did. It's a relief. I don't have to hide from you. I finally have someone I can trust."

"You trust me?" Her voice came out as a squeak.

Black reached into the cab and slid his hand around the back of her head, his thumb caressing the cup of her ear. "I showed you my shift. If that's not trust, I don't know what is. Plus you're fun to do naughty things to."

She flushed, the butterflies in her stomach sending a giggle up her throat. "But what about life-mates and all that?"

His teasing smile grew serious. He leaned in to brush his lips against hers, and his breath was warm and sweet. "This centaur's found his."

*B*lack hung a new IV from the barn rafter above Ivy-Jane, feeling the weight of Lori's gaze on his back. The foal lay with three legs curled beneath her, the fourth, wrapped in a bandage, stuck out straight in front of her. The sprain would be fine in a few days if he could keep her off her feet. But right now the foal was the least of his worries.

Renee had returned to the house, needing rest after all she'd learned, and he was glad she wasn't around to overhear Lori's hateful words. Black turned to face the herd leader, her heeled boots bringing her to eye level. Saul sat on a nearby straw bale his face an emotionless mask.

"The deal was I'd marry her. " Black clenched his fists to keep his anger under control. "And I will. Just give me more than two days to do it, for Christ's sake."

He wanted nothing more than to build a life with Renee. She said she needed time to think, and he could give her that. After all, she'd been hit with a lot of new information in a short period of time. Hell, so had he. Being with her had made him reconsider his life goals. He didn't need rank in the herd anymore, as long as he could have Renee. The relief he'd felt showing her his shift had almost been as satisfying as the ecstasy he'd felt buried in her pussy. Almost. The idea of having a life-mate, having someone he didn't have to hide from or pretend to be someone else around, made his blood sing. For the first time since discovering he'd never be able to fully shift, he felt alive. If it took him an entire lifetime, he'd use it to make Renee his.

"It's too late for that." Lori stood wide, hands on hips.

He blinked, coming back to reality. "She's not going to expose us."

"Oh, after two sweaty interludes you know her so well?" Lori cocked one manicured eyebrow.

Black glared at the barn wall where he pictured Millie on the other side, skulking like a little rat. The mare had obviously told Lori about this morning. "I do—"

"She's here to sell the place," Lori interrupted. "She told me so the first day she arrived."

Refusing to back down, Black stalked past her and Saul toward the cubbies where spare boots and clothes were kept. "She might've intended to sell when she first got here, but I bet she doesn't now."

"That girl is out for money. I've seen her kind before. If she doesn't sell the place, she'll certainly exploit us."

"Just because you would, doesn't mean Renee will." He could trust Renee—the herd could trust her—just as his grandma had trusted Toliman.

"We're out of time, soldier. And protecting the herd is paramount. We've got enough witnesses to forge the marriage documents." Lori's voice dropped to a threatening purr. "And once we get her to sign them, we'll take her out for one last ride."

Shock froze Black in place. Lori hadn't said it directly, but the meaning was clear. The words reminded him of the way she'd pretended to grieve her predecessor's death. *Gloryanna died giving her human one last ride.* Lori was proposing murder. The murder of his mate. Slowly, Black turned to face the herd leader, mind still trying to accept the truth.

Saul rose ponderously, shaking his head. "Her family will protest. We'd likely lose the ranch in probate."

Lori rolled her eyes. "The only family she has left is her religious-fanatic father, and he thinks this place is cursed. Believe me, I've thought this through."

Saul scrubbed both hands through his wild, black hair. "Killing her seems a little extreme."

"No one's killing anyone." Black's voice was a low growl, as if his animal nature was more bear-like than equine.

"Keep your voice down," Lori warned. "It's the perfect plan. And I don't care which one of you is the groom. I just need an extra witness signature on the papers. Saul, you on board?"

Saul hesitated a moment, then asked, "Millie and Su are in agreement?"

Black stiffened. "You can't be considering this?"

Saul refused to meet his gaze. "She's just a human."

"She's not just a human. She's my mate. And she's Toliman's granddaughter," Black gestured toward the direction of the house. "Is this how you repay him for years of protecting the herd? By murdering his only grandchild and stealing his ranch?"

At least Saul had the grace to blush. Lori stepped between Black and his uncle, shimmering as if on the verge of a shift. "Don't be stupid. Humans can't be mates. The herd comes first. I should've known better than to expect you to understand that."

Her words stung like the lash of a whip. But Black'd had enough. Shifter magic tingled across his skin. "I look out for this herd just as much or more than you do. My grandmother was Lead Mare, and one thing I know is Renee is my life-mate. I'm calling a herd meeting."

She scowled. "You can't call a herd meeting. You barely even have rank."

Saul's gaze shifted between Lori and Black. "Any shifter can call a herd meeting."

"Like they'll listen to a centaur." She snorted derisively. "Besides, it's almost daylight. You might be seen."

The tingle subsided as Black realized she was right. He couldn't go out as a centaur.

Crackling tires on gravel cut short the conversation. Lori bared her teeth. "Fuck. She said she had a realtor coming today. We need to get rid of him."

She spun toward the door and stalked out. Black and Saul followed close behind. In the heavy sunshine, a shiny new Dodge Ram with a Wright Minerals Co. logo on the door was rolling to a stop in front of the house, heat waves warping the air over its hood.

Lori slowed her pace, and Black spared her a glance as he passed her. Usually she insisted on being the face of the ranch, but maybe she was too angry and flustered to deal with it right now.

The engine silenced, and a man slid from the cab, adjusting a black Stetson over his balding head. He gave Black a thousand-watt smile. "Afternoon. I'm looking for Lori Sandvur."

"Lori?" Black glanced at her, confused.

Lori had her hands on her hips, glowering. "You're not supposed to be here until next week."

"I'm in the area and thought I'd take a quick look," the guy said.

She stepped forward, stopping abreast of Black. "Turn around and leave. Now."

The man held his palms up, looking from Lori to Black to Saul. Uncle Saul just stood there, thumbs in the loops of his jeans. Black narrowed his eyes at Lori. Why'd she contacted a mining company?

"I apologize, ma'am." The man backed to his truck. "I'll be in contact next week."

Quick as an arrow, Black was at the truck door, hand flat against the window frame to keep it closed. He wanted this story straight from the source, not Lori's convoluted version. "Why don't you tell us what you'll be in contact about?"

Scratching the back of his neck, the man glanced at Lori, then back to Black. "Ms. Sandvur sent in a rock sample several months back. Seems there's gold on the property, and she has some questions about getting it out of the ground."

Black dropped his hand and spun toward the lead mare. Gold? When had that happened? News of gold would bring a lot of attention to the ranch. Human attention. What was the lead mare thinking? Behind her, Saul's mouth hung open.

Lori crossed her arms and settled her weight on one leg, gaze still on the visitor. "I told you to leave, mister."

The guy shook his head and jerked open the truck door. "Next time I'm bringing backup," he muttered as he slammed the door shut. The engine rumbled to life and the man gunned the truck into reverse down the driveway.

Black let him go. The man wasn't the issue. In silence, he watched the truck round the base of the hill before speaking again. This time he turned to Saul. "You said the buried treasure was the herd."

Saul shook his head. "It was. At least as far as I understood." He moved up to stand next to Lori, his brows drawn into a frown. "What's this about gold?"

Lori shot a look toward the house and spun, boots crunching over the gravel as she bee-lined toward the barn. "The ranch can't sustain itself without income. I'm trying to see to the herd's future."

"Wait, there really is gold?" Black lengthened his stride to keep up, a twitch irritating his left eye. Why hadn't Lori mentioned the find before?

Inside the barn, Lori entered the nearest stall. She spun to face the men, her voice a whisper. "In the canyon where Toliman died."

"Did he know about it?" Black didn't bother to keep quiet.

She bared her teeth at him and focused on Saul, as if Black didn't matter. "The gold will give us freedom like the herd's never known, not since before the settlers fenced everything off. Once we've secured the land deed—"

The soft tread of feet outside was followed by, "Black?"

Lori hissed, her fingernails biting into his arm. "Don't you dare say a thing, Black."

"It's her land. Her gold." He jerked free, Lori's nails leaving long welts on his skin. Turning, he strode toward the bay door.

Within three steps, he felt the air behind him swirl and condense with shifter magic. Lori's pale palomino form bowled past him, knocking him to the side. He tripped over a stall rake leaning against the wall, the handle tangling his legs. He fell to his hands and knees, palms jarring against the gravel. Saul's bulky equine shape followed close behind Lori, disappearing out the barn door.

Black struggled to his feet, his shift grabbing hold of every muscle in his body, straining the seams of his clothing and boots as he shouted, "Renee, look out!"

A sleek blonde palomino careened out of the barn toward Renee, a terrifying scream issuing from between its bared teeth. Startled, Renee fell backward, landing with a painful thump on her backside. Head lowered, the horse churned up bits of gravel, charging straight at her. Renee rolled, flinging herself out of the way. Hooves streaked within a hair's breadth of her shoulder. The beast's momentum slowed as it rounded the driveway. It then faced her again, ears pinned, and reared.

A bolt of fear ricocheted through Renee's blood. *Is it angry at me?*

Before she could react, a familiar charcoal-gray stallion barreled out the door. *Uncle Saul?* Renee clambered to her feet, palms stinging from the gravel. The stallion drew up facing the mare, neck arched and teeth bared. *Were they fighting? What was going on?*

Yet another form exited the barn. Renee let out a breath of relief to see Black's centaur shape gleaming magnificently in the sun, bare torso rippling with muscle. He pounded toward Renee, and she backed up a step, uncertain. Thrusting a hand toward her, he commanded, "Get on."

The seriousness of his gaze gave her strength, and she gripped his hand. He lifted her with a powerful flex of his arm, settling her into the curve where horse met man.

"Hold tight," he said, and spun toward the fence gate.

"Is that Lori?" Renee wrapped her arms around his chest, glancing at the gaping barn door in case any more rabid horses decided to emerge.

"Yes," he gritted between clenched teeth, freeing the gate latch.

Glancing over her shoulder, Renee sucked in a breath as the palomino reared back, front hooves churning the air. The stallion reared in return. They clashed, teeth gnashing and front legs flailing.

Black lurched forward, and Renee was forced to face front again, wrapping both arms tightly around his ribcage. *I'm riding a centaur. Again.* The thought would have made her giddy if she wasn't already dizzy with confusion. Pressing her cheek to his shoulder blade, she squeezed her knees around his withers to hold herself steady. Within moments, he was at a canter, headed for the road toward town, and Renee found herself easily adjusting to the rhythm of his gait. The combination of man and beast felt so natural, she closed her eyes, enjoying the passing air, the feel of his muscles flexing beneath her, the warm scent of his skin.

Her brief dip into sensuality was broken by pounding hooves approaching on the left. Her eyes popped open to see the palomino giving chase. Even more horrifying, the beast's pale muzzle was flecked with blood.

"Black!" Renee cried.

Leaning forward, Black increased speed, but the palomino continued to gain. The mare reached his hind quarters, neck stretching forward and lips drawn back in almost predatory ferocity. Renee could swear the horse's eyes glowed with demonic light.

At that moment, Black grabbed painfully tight to Renee's thighs, and it felt like his hind legs went out from under him. Turning sharply, he skidded to a stop.

Too terrified to even scream, Renee hung on for dear life.

The palomino overshot them, hooves scrambling against the parched grass. Black looked over his shoulder into Renee's eyes. "You okay?"

She nodded, her voice still caught in her throat.

"This might get ugly. Whatever happens, get as far away from Lori as you can, okay?"

Renee watched the mare paw the ground. Lori was horrible in human form. As a horse, she seemed possessed. "What's wrong with her?"

Black shook his head, dancing sideways as the mare stalked toward them with her neck arched menacingly. Renee locked her hands around his chest as he angled his upper body to shield her from the mare. Lori tossed her head, white mane flaring wildly. Then she lunged, that awful sound screeching from her throat.

Black grasped Renee's thighs like before and reared, pummeling Lori with his front hooves.

Clinging to him for dear life, Renee pressed her cheek flat against his shoulder blade, heartbeat racing ahead of her breathing. With every ounce of strength, she squeezed her knees to keep her seat. Black's muscles rippled and flexed between her legs, and she felt herself sliding loose in spite of his added grip on her thighs.

The mare backed away, and Black dropped back to all fours with a jarring thud. Renee wriggled to regain her seat.

Then the mare twisted, ninja fast, lashing out with her back legs.

Black dodged right.

Deadly hooves cut the air where Renee's thigh had been.

With lightning speed, Lori sprang forward again, sending Black into a backward leap. Renee wobbled precariously. Black threw a hand back to steady her, and Lori took advantage of the distraction, lunging again.

This time, teeth bit into Renee's leg just above the knee. Renee cried out in pain, muscle bruised against bone. The next thing she knew, her grip tore free of Black's chest and she was flying through the air. She landed hard on the dirt, her left shoulder taking the brunt of the impact.

Dust-choked air burning her lungs, she rolled to her knees. The ground shook with beating hooves while Lori and Black continued their battle. Black kept himself between Renee and the mare, but Lori was ferocious, biting and kicking until blood streaked Black's bare chest and arms.

Another twisting kick caught Black's cheek. He reeled, hooves stuttering unevenly across the ground. Lori broke away, and a horrific realization struck Renee. This fight wasn't between herd members. It wasn't about Lori and Black. *He's protecting* me.

Renee hopped sideways, trying to get away. Her bitten knee throbbed. Her left arm tingled from her fall. She couldn't get away, but she could fight back. Searching the ground, she located a stone the size of a softball. She hurled it at the oncoming mare as hard as she could.

The palomino shied away, bucking her hind legs as if to kick the stone from the air. In one fluid movement, she rounded on Renee again, whites of her eyes gleaming. Both front hooves pawed the air.

Black threw himself into Lori's path. "Run, Renee!"

Renee limped back another step while the mare snapped her teeth. Black caught the bite with his forearm, shoving the palomino's bulk backward. His front hooves slashed the palomino's chest, drawing bloody grooves into her pale hide.

Renee scoured the ground for another rock. No way was she leaving Black to fight this bitch alone. The pasture here was frustratingly clear of stones. Several yards to her left, a handful of horses had appeared. They stood watching curiously, tails swishing the dusty air. Were they shifters? Why were they just standing around?

Black threw his arms around the palomino's throat. His biceps bulged as their horse bodies scrambled for dominance. Lori managed a well-aimed kick against his hind leg and he went down, dragging her head along with him. The mare's neck muscles stood out as she tried bucking off his added weight.

A chocolate brown horse in the nearby herd tossed its head and whinnied, looking at the nearby lane. The other horses nickered and looked that direction. A second later Renee heard it, too—the thrum of an approaching engine. *Oh, God, the realtor.* She'd never canceled the appointment.

A small white sedan appeared around the hill, moving

slowly toward the house. It disappeared at a low spot in the road, but within seconds it would appear again, in full view of the fight.

"Black!" Renee cried. "A car's coming!"

He'd wrestled Lori to the ground and knelt with both forelegs against her neck, his hands on her head. He couldn't hear her.

She had to stop that car. Lurching toward the fence, she shimmied between the rails. Maybe she could stop the realtor before he saw anything. Block his view. Distract him. Anything. After a few steps, her injured knee gave out. She landed with both palms on the gravel, fire lancing through her wrists. Refusing to stop, she scrambled upright and limped down the gravel lane.

The car skidded to a stop amidst clouds of dust. Through the windshield, Renee watched the young man's mouth form a perfect circle, his gaze focused past her on Black and Lori. *Shit shit shit!* She reached the car door, and the realtor rolled the window down a crack. His voice tremored. "Is everything all right?"

Shooting a glance toward the fight, Renee was surprised to see six or eight naked people in a circle around Black. He knelt on the mare's neck in human form. "Uh," she said, unsure how to respond. Like a lightbulb, her father's accusations about dark rituals and voodoo came to her. She smiled and leaned toward the window. "It's a spiritual ceremony. Religious. Everything's fine."

"Oh." The realtor cleared his throat, his gaze flicking down to Renee's bleeding hands. "How about I come back later?"

Renee shook her head, closing her fingers over the stinging wounds. "I've changed my mind about selling the place. Sorry you drove all the way out here."

The man nodded, already shifting into reverse. "Not a problem. Really. I'm... you... have a great day."

She stood up, allowing the man to escape the unnaturally still scene outside. He gunned the accelerator all the way back down the driveway. Once the car had disappeared around the hill, she returned her attention to the herd of people assembled around Black. This was her ranch, and she was done being pushed around.

13

Black gulped air, kneeling with his full weight on Lori's carotid artery. Renee's voice only reached him through a fog. His full attention remained on the twitching horse. He'd made it into human form in time to avoid being seen, but without his centaur's weight bearing her down, Lori would regain control any moment. Sure enough, she rolled, forcing him to scramble away from her crushing weight.

The car's retreating engine hadn't yet reached the road as Lori regained her feet, eyes rolling with fury. Immediately she reared, razor sharp hooves churning the air. Although Renee was on the other side of the fence, Lori could clear that in mere steps.

153

Fuck this, Black thought. He no longer cared if he was seen. No longer cared if the herd saw him shift. His life-mate was in danger. Still in human form, he charged, tightening the shifter magic into a ball inside him then letting it flash outward in an explosion of change.

He reached the fence in centaur form at almost the same moment as Lori, his full weight tackling her off balance. Her front legs cleared the rail, but her back legs hit hard, knocking the wood beam loose. She and the rail tumbled head over feet into the gravel, raising a choking cloud of dust.

Renee had retreated to the other side of the lane and now stood with her back pressed to the fence on that side.

Black cleared the damaged fence, shooting past Lori and skidding to a halt between his mate and the mare.

Lori writhed in the gravel, her high-pitched screeching putting his teeth on edge. Glinting white bone poked like a spear from her right hind leg. Black's vet instincts reared up, but he resisted the urge to help. If this was what it took to stop Lori, so be it. A break that bad would likely cripple her for life, since pins and other hardware used to fix broken limbs didn't play well with shifter physiology.

The rest of the herd, still in human form, ducked through the fence and approached, gazes flickering between Black and their lead mare.

All Black could think about was getting Renee out of here, to safety, even if that meant parading his centaur form straight into town. He knelt on the gravel next to Renee. "Can you ride?"

She crossed her arms. "I could. But I won't. This is my ranch, and I'm not being chased off." Putting a hand on his wither, she nudged him aside and stepped out to face the oncoming shifters. "As the new owner of this ranch, I call a herd meeting."

Black watched her in astonishment, a proud smile tugging the corners of his lips. The shifters slowed, standing in a line on the opposite side of their lead mare. Lori's shrieking stopped, and her golden body shimmered and shrank, hooves becoming feet and hands, mane transforming into mussed blonde hair. Bone still poked from her bloody shin, and her face was a rictus of pain. Through gritted teeth, she yelled, "This human can't call a herd meeting."

More shifters arrived, still in horse form. The ones in human form murmured among themselves as the newcomers shifted. This was a good sign. For once they weren't obeying Lori on pure fear and instinct. Black squared his shoulders. What he was about to do was more nerve wracking than showing Renee his shift. "Renee's my life-mate. I demand the protection of the herd."

The word "life-mate" whispered through the crowd. Black watched Renee out of the corner of his eye, unsure what her reaction might be to this announcement. She gawked at him, a huge question behind her eyes. But he didn't have time to get down on one knee and ask if she felt the same.

Lori had bared her teeth, lips quivering. "She's a danger to the herd."

Renee placed her hands on her hips, her stance wide and assured. "I'm not the one who started this fight. And I'd appreciate someone telling me what the hell is going on." She looked up at Black. "Why's she trying to kill me?"

He glared at Lori as he answered. "The treasure in your grandfather's will is real."

"I thought you said the treasure was the horses?" Renee waved at the surrounding crowd of shifters. "And by that, I assume you meant the shifter herd."

"I did. And I think your grandfather thought they were, too." He curled his lip in disgust at Lori. "But apparently Lori found gold in the canyon."

Renee's eyes widened. "Really? I'm... I still don't understand, though. Why attack me?"

Black's eyes were drawn to Renee's blood-flecked pant-leg, and his pulse thundered again. He shifted to human form and knelt beside her. "Let me look at that. Are you all right?"

"Unless she has rabies or something, I'll be fine." Renee batted at his hand. "Tell me why she wants me dead."

Black refused to let go of her leg, examining the wound. Let Lori try to defend herself. "Care to share your plans with the herd, Lori?"

The blonde curled her lips in a feral snarl. Even though Lori couldn't possibly stand on a broken leg and attack, a few of the nearby onlookers backed away a step. "You can't trust a human."

Millie ducked her head from between two of the men and raised her hand. She didn't say anything, just stood there with her hand up. Black narrowed his eyes, uncertain about her sudden boldness. But she wasn't looking at Black. She was looking at Renee.

"What's your name?" Renee asked.

"Millie," the woman rasped.

"Ivy-Jane's mother?" Renee glanced at Black, who nodded.

Satisfied Renee's wound wasn't critical, he rose and asked, "Millie, what do you know about this?"

"Lori murdered Toliman and Gloryanna." Millie ducked back between the men as if expecting a blow.

A collective gasp rose among the group. Lori glowered but said nothing.

Black's blood turned cold. *Murdered?* The air had become too thick to breathe. He'd always suspected foul play, but by one of his own herd-mates? Poor Grandma probably never saw anything coming. His throat tightened. "Why?"

Lori snarled. "I'm the one who found the gold. I begged Toliman to have the ore tested. He just wanted to let it sit there while we slaved away keeping his precious ranch running. I would have used the money for the herd. We'd never worry about our security again."

"So you killed him?" Renee's voice came out an octave too high. "How did you think killing him—killing me—would make the gold yours?"

An evil look entered Lori's eyes. "Ask your so-called life-mate." She smirked at Black. "You don't have to play the part anymore, Black. The cat's out of the bag."

Black glowered at Lori, nostrils flaring, heart thumping hard against his ribs. Of course she'd try to get in one final blow.

"What's she talking about?" Renee asked.

Lori's voice dripped saccharine-laced poison. "Black was going to convince you to marry him, sweetie."

The full weight of what he stood to lose by telling Renee the truth slammed into him. A life-mate was a rare gift, one not many shifters found. But he couldn't lie to her, even if it meant losing her forever. Renee's eyes glittered with pain, but he pressed on. "When you first arrived, I agreed to marry you in return for a rank in the herd."

"You'll never have that now." Lori interjected. "You know that, don't you?"

Black ignored her, his eyes only for Renee, pleading for her to understand. "The plan wasn't to hurt you. Only to keep you from selling the ranch. And you're so beautiful, it was easy to pursue you. But then you saw me. You saw my... monster." The words felt thick in Black's throat, but he kept on. "And you accepted me."

"You're not a monster," Renee said softly.

He grit his teeth, refusing to look away from Renee's trusting gaze. *A monster like you doesn't deserve a life-mate.* "I am a monster. I agreed to Lori's initial plan to steal your inheritance. I think she planned to kill you all along, but I refused to see it."

"But you defended me." Renee shook her head. "And we're not married. How would killing me now make the ranch Lori's?"

"She was going to forge the marriage papers and claim the ranch in probate. When I found out, I refused." The plan still made Black sick to his stomach. He didn't mention that Saul had considered the deal. After all, his uncle had thrown himself at Lori and given Black time to grab Renee and try to escape. Black still didn't know what had made his uncle change his mind, but he would be forever grateful.

Lori curled her lips. "I'm the only one strong enough to do what's best for the herd."

Renee's mouth became a thin, pale line, and in spite of her diminutive height, she seemed to stand ten feet tall. "Best for the herd? You have no idea what that even means." She looked at Black, eyes burning with dark fire, then swiveled to address the crowd. "I don't know most of you, but I'm going to assume you're good people. Black's people. This woman murdered my grandfather and Black's grandmother—your previous leader. What's the herd punishment for murderers?"

To Black's surprise, the shifters dipped their heads in respect. He had to admit, the commanding force radiating off Renee at the moment rivaled that of his grandmother. *Grandma.* Lori had killed her. His veins felt sluggish with ice, reliving the loss.

One of the bachelors spoke up. "Banishment is customary."

"Banishment?" Renee drew up straighter and crossed her arms. "So she can find another herd to terrorize? I don't think so."

Black wanted to string Lori from the nearest tree, but that punishment would be better than she deserved.

She'd murdered two people. Terrorized the herd. And tried to kill his life mate. He wanted a punishment that would make her suffer. He glanced at her shattered leg and realized she'd already done that to herself. "Her days of running with a herd are over."

Lori's face paled to a chalky white. She stared at her leg as if only now realizing the break was real.

"Because of her leg?" asked Renee. "Can't she just have surgery?"

"She could." Black knelt next to Lori, his vet instincts breaking through his anger. The break looked even worse up close. "But the bolts and other hardware used to fix it would detach the first time she tried to shift. She'd be worse off than she is now. And without surgery, she'll be crippled for life. In both forms." Black kept his gaze on Lori, trying to find satisfaction at the thought of her crippled. It wasn't enough, but it would have to do.

Renee's eyes brimmed with tears, but the hard lines on her face told him she was angry, not feeling empathy. "I don't know if that's enough. But this isn't only about me." She spoke with that same note of authority she'd used when she'd asked about punishment earlier. She looked at the people around her, making Black take notice of them, too. Bachelors. Elders. Mothers. Teens.

His herd. She said, "You lost someone, too. And it sounds like there's still a choice to be made. Does she have surgery or not? How does the herd vote?"

"Wait!" Lori begged the watching shifters. "My plan could still work. There's no one here but us. Just say the word—"

A bachelor walked past Lori without sparing her a glance and placed a hand gently on Renee's shoulder. Then he turned to face the watching shifters. A gray-haired elder stepped closer and took Renee's hand. Slowly, the entire herd moved to surround Renee and Black in the kind of acceptance only a herd could give.

Pride blossomed in Black's chest. They were affirming his life-mate. Not even Old Man Toliman had received this kind of acceptance. He'd been respected, and the herd loved him, but he'd always been an outsider. A benefactor, not a peer. Renee had just become both.

An elder woman raised her voice. "She doesn't deserve an equine form. I say surgery."

"Take her to the human hospital."

"Put in pins."

"You can't!" Lori screamed as two bachelors stepped forward, grabbing her by the arms. "They won't operate without my consent!"

One of the men shook his head. "Not if you arrive unconscious."

Her face creased into ugly lines. "I'm your lead mare! I was only looking out for you!"

The men dragged a screaming Lori from the pasture. They'd handle her from here, and Black was relieved to be free of the duty. Most of the shifters followed in human form. Others shimmered to horse form and departed toward the pasture.

Black only had eyes for Renee. He rubbed a hand over his hair, missing the comfortable weight of his cowboy hat. "How's your leg? I can carry you home if you don't mind riding bareback."

She looked at him through her lashes. "Mmm. Riding a cowboy bareback. I like it."

He chuckled, pleased to see his flirty little filly back. Kneeling next to her, he helped steady her as she lifted her injured leg over his flanks. Once she was settled in place, he rose. Her warmth settled against his spine, and her legs wrapped his withers with a comforting pressure he'd never expected to feel with a rider. Shifters talked about how humiliating it was to carry a human, how uncomfortable and heavy. But he rather liked how close it drew Renee against him. She wrapped her arms around his chest and settled her cheek against his shoulder with a sigh, her breath wafting across his bare skin.

He eased into a level trot, heading toward the ranch. Her knees tightened around him, ignoring the pain from the bite. "I want to feel the wind. Will you run for me?"

His blood thrilled at the words. "Are you sure?"

Her cheek nodded yes against his back. "I love you like this."

He bunched his hind quarters and took off at a canter. Renee clung tightly to him, her body moving with his, melding against his, in an act as intimate as sex.

They passed Lori, who spat obscenities at them, but Black kept going. Renee cried, "Faster!"

"Don't let go!" He yelled back.

"Never!"

He veered left, skirting the fence, and kicked it up to a gallop. Her thighs pressed his flanks, her breath hot on his shoulder. He'd never felt so free. So alive. He let out a whoop of joy, echoed by her laughter behind him. Taking a wide arc, he headed back to the house at a trot. If he never had anything else in this world, he had this moment, this inkling of belonging to someone, and he'd nurture the feeling the rest of his life.

EPILOGUE

*R*enee played her fingers across Black's chest, traced her lips over the line of his shoulder as he trotted over the darkened pasture. Crickets sang their nightly serenade from among the rocks where they'd first made love. She delighted in his sweet hay scent and this land.

Her land. Her ranch. The idea was still so new, she sometimes woke thinking she must've dreamed the whole thing. She'd been here over a week, overseeing everything from daily stall-mucking to a secret shifter meeting beneath a midnight moon. So much of her dad's misconceptions about her grandfather made sense now. Maybe she should reach out to him now that she was settling down...

Black reached back and brushed a hand up her leg. "You okay?"

He somehow knew what she was thinking and feeling almost as soon as she did these days. She didn't understand how he could know her so well in such a short time, but she knew she was happy here with him. Whole.

"I'm good," she said, rubbing her cheek against his back. Whatever was going on inside her, she hadn't figured out how to talk about it yet.

He seemed to know that, too, and continued on, his hooves thudding softly against the earth, steady as a heartbeat. Renee realized that what had been dancing around in her mind had nothing to do with her father, her mother, or even her grandfather. What she needed to talk about was right here on the ranch. Right here in her arms. *Life-mate.* They hadn't talked about it since he first told the herd. As though he knew it scared her more than any thrill-seeking she'd done with Steph.

But now she was ready to jump.

Taking a breath, she tightened her arms around Black's ribcage. "Will you marry me? For real?"

Another corny line, she realized, too late to take it back.

Black stopped and craned his neck to look at her, his lips crooked in a sideways smile. "You're not just playing me, are you?"

She grinned impishly. He really did understand her. "I've never been very good at pick up lines, so I figured I'd cut to the chase. Besides, you did call me your life-mate, right?"

His face turned solemn. With one deft move, he lifted her from his back and set her gently to the ground before shimmering back to human form. "You are my life-mate, Renee. I love you. I have nothing to offer you but myself and a promise of undying adoration and protection. But if you'll be my bride, I pledge myself to you freely and fully, until death steals my last breath."

Renee took a step closer. "I don't know how you did it, but you changed me." She swallowed. "I love you, Black."

He looked down into her eyes. "You changed me, too."

Sliding one hand around her neck, he cupped her head and drew her into a kiss. She linked her hands around his waist and pressed her heartbeat next to his. She'd finally found the one thrill she was willing to die for. And the only one she wanted to repeat every day for the rest of her life.

*D*ear Reader,

Thank you for reading The Centaur's Bride. Craving more sweet and steamy shifter romance? You'll love my Alaska Alphas series because it features characters you'll fall in love with. Book one, Untamed Instinct, starts with an outcast shifter who wanders the Alaskan wilderness alone—until he saves a witch's life. Can their forbidden love find a happily ever after?

Keep reading for a sneak peek!

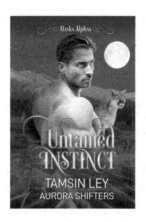

UNTAMED INSTINCT

SNEAK PEEK

*A*drian crouched among the cottonwood leaves, claws digging into the bark as he surveyed the dead moose in the clearing below. He'd been waiting here in his mountain lion form for several hours and was eager to move on, but had to be certain the carcass had been deserted before he drew closer to investigate. He'd received numerous reports of abandoned animal kills over the last few weeks, and his supervisor at the ranger station wanted whoever—or whatever—was doing the poaching to be tracked down.

Scattered throughout the Wrangell-St. Elias Park, the previous sites had been old before Adrian reached them, the evidence around the carcasses obscured by smaller predators and decay. This site seemed fresher, the stench of rot less intense, although flies swarmed over the bull's hide and stubby, velvet-covered antlers. If the killer was human, they weren't out for trophies. And they definitely weren't doing it for meat. Someone or something was killing for fun, and they were slowly moving closer to human-occupied lands.

Adrian's tail twitched angrily, and he let out a grunt of resignation before dropping nimbly to the ground. The scent of rotting flesh grew stronger as he approached, and flies rose in a cloud, exposing gashes writhing with fresh maggots.

He circled the moose, estimating it had been dead slightly longer than twenty-four hours. Clawed paw prints, almost twice the size of his own, scarred the earth around the kill. He lowered his muzzle and sniffed, tail lashing. The familiar musk of a grizzly filled his nose. *Shifter grizzly.* He released a hiss of displeasure. The last thing the shifter community wanted was a rogue member drawing attention to the national park. Randall, Adrian's tough-as-nails wolf supervisor, would not like this.

Fuck, Adrian didn't like it either. Mountain lions weren't unheard of in Alaska, but rare enough to cause a ruckus among humans if sighted. The vast wilds of the park were his refuge—his *territory* in the mind of his mountain lion. The local bear shifters would want to take care of a rogue grizzly themselves.

Adrian exposed his canines and turned away, prowling through the trees toward his ranger cabin to call his supervisor.

Just out of sight of his cabin, he shifted and retrieved the uniform he kept in a hollow tree, shrugging into his clothing before emerging into the clearing. His cabin was a small log building nestled next to one of the many rock faces jutting from the mountain, roof covered in thick moss and a small porch screened in from mosquitoes. One of the more popular trailheads started nearby, and a small message board fluttered with notices campers left to each other at the end of his overgrown driveway.

Inside the two-room cabin, a few small windows shed dusky light over the sparse furnishings. Passing the small front area with a table, a propane fridge, a wood stove, and an old sofa, he moved to the bedroom where a king-sized bed took up almost every inch of space. He retrieved his cell phone from the nightstand and moved to the corner of the front room where he got the best reception. He kept an old ham radio in the shed for when the notoriously spotty cell service didn't work, but he couldn't talk to Randall about shifter business over the radio. Thankfully, the phone showed two bars today. He dialed the main ranger office.

"This is HQ," a woman's nasal voice answered.

"Cherry, it's Adrian. I need to talk to Randall."

"Oh, hi, handsome!" Her voice brightened. "We haven't heard from you in a while. How've you been?"

Adrian bared his teeth and reminded himself to be polite; Cherry was human. "Doing fine."

He hated social niceties, which was why he'd become a ranger in the first place. This remote location suited him well, and he only ventured into town when he needed supplies. Most of his duties allowed him to patrol the trails alone, talking to the occasional hiker and reporting any problems. Several times a year he had to oversee search and rescue operations when a hiker got lost, but more often than not, he found the missing person before a full team even arrived.

"You doing okay on handouts?" Cherry chirped back.

He glanced toward the door where a stack of papers had gathered a layer of dust. He was supposed to pass them out to tourists, but since he avoided people, he used very few. "All good. I just need to talk to Randall."

"You betcha."

The phone clicked. A few heartbeats later, the supervisor's voice came on the line. "Adrian, what's up?"

"I've got a lead on the poacher. I found a spike-fork moose abandoned yesterday, and there's fresh grizzly sign all over the place. Smells like a shifter."

"Shit. Don't tell me the infection's moved to our territory."

"What infection?"

"Rogues." The sound of fingernails against beard stubble scratched over the phone line. "Two rogue wolves and a moose were put down in Anchorage over the winter, then a black bear outside Valdez this spring. No rhyme or reason to why. Council sent out a memo a while back. Don't you read your emails, Adrian?"

Adrian glanced at the dust-covered laptop under the nightstand. "Not like I have wifi out here, Randall. I'll catch up next time I go into town."

Randall made a frustrated noise over the phone. "Well, if a shifter's behind these abandoned kills, it's likely a rogue. File your report then go handle it ASAP."

"Me? Isn't this Den business?" Although the Council oversaw shifter law, local shifter groups liked to take care of their own business.

"Not this time. A travel blogger already posted about the kills. We need to get ahead of the news before it goes viral. Take your rifle."

"I'm a ranger, not a SWAT team, Randall."

"This is your territory. I need you to handle it. There could be hikers in danger."

"Fuck." Adrian grimaced. "What if he shifts before he dies?" It was one thing for a ranger to take down a dangerous bear. Quite another if a human body showed up killed by a ranger's bullet. And in a face-to-face fight, a mountain lion couldn't stand up to a full-grown grizzly, especially a shifter gone rogue.

"Make your first shot count."

"I hate this shit." Hanging up, Adrian pocketed his phone and grabbed his rifle before heading back outside. He'd file a report when he got back. Best to get on the trail while it was still relatively warm.

He started up his ATV, its disused engine letting out a disgusting belch of smoke. The damn thing cut off his ability to hear or smell anything, which made his mountain lion bristle in discomfort. *I know, me too.* But he couldn't carry his rifle while in feline form.

Stowing the weapon in the mounted case on the front of the ATV, he rolled out of the cabin's clearing toward the trailhead parking lot.

CHAPTER TWO

Darcy stopped her Subaru and eyed the overgrown path. According to Google, this dirt road should lead to a trailhead parking lot, but it looked like if she drove any farther, she might end up "parked" more permanently. Her all-wheel drive had managed the old, rutted road, but the path was getting narrower, with branches rubbing her door panels. *Did I take a wrong turn?*

She glanced in her rearview mirror. There had been a space wide enough to turn around a short way back. Putting the car in reverse, she carefully maneuvered through the brush, backing into a flat area that looked like it would make a nice campsite.

The overcast sky filtered dimly through the thick canopy of trees, and she hadn't seen a soul since turning into what had started out as a fairly decent dirt road. She rolled down her window and breathed in the verdant forest air. *This looks like as good a place to start as any.*

Her interview with the coven was the day after tomorrow, and she'd come in search of herbs to make an eloquence potion. This would be her last-ditch effort to overcome the stutter that ruined every spell she tried to cast. Poor Aunt Willow still had a patch of white hair behind one ear from one of her lessons. Darcy'd tried to buy an eloquence potion from the local apothecary shop, but it turned out it only worked for the person who made it, and the effects would not be permanent. But she didn't need to be *good* at incantations, only steady enough to pass the coven's apprenticeship test.

Cutting the engine, she reached over to the passenger seat to retrieve her copy of *Wild Edible and Medicinal Plants of the Pacific Northwest*. She was more familiar with gardens than wilderness, but her mom had sent her to summer camp every year of her childhood, and the forest didn't daunt her.

Tapping her phone, she opened her GPS app and pinned her current location so she could find her way back, then tucked it and the book into a reusable grocery bag alongside a small trowel, a pair of purple and yellow gardening gloves, and a compact rain poncho. She looked around as she stepped out of the car, taking in a circle of stones around an overgrown fire pit. The mossy log seats around it obviously hadn't been disturbed in quite a while, and knee-high saplings and brush filled the clearing.

Locking the car even though she doubted she needed to, she headed toward what looked like a trail on the uphill side of the clearing. According to her book, wild rhodiola rosea grew on rocky slopes at high altitudes.

She set off between the trees, scanning the surrounding plants for signs of fleshy rhodiola leaves. A thick layer of dry leaves and twigs crunched under her feet, birds sang overhead, and in the distance a woodpecker tatted out a rhythm. She let out a contented sigh, running her fingertips over the smooth gray trunk of a quaking aspen as she passed.

A scraggly thicket of salmonberries crowded the trail, and she sampled a few, letting the sweet juice coat her tongue. A mosquito buzzed her ear, and she reached into her bag for her homemade insect repellant. She wasn't yet much good at magical potions, but she had a decent grasp of essential oils, and her minty-citrus concoction not only worked, it smelled good. After dousing herself, she tucked the small spray bottle away and continued on.

The path grew steeper, making her calves burn as she climbed until she reached a sharp turn. To her right, the trail paralleled the top of a rocky ridge, but about fifteen feet below, she spotted a clump of rosette shaped leaves. *Rhodiola?* She stepped toward the edge to get a better look.

The ground beneath her feet collapsed. Too startled to even scream, she bumped and slithered helplessly down the incline on her backside, coming to a stop among a rain of pebbles and dust.

More stunned than hurt, she sat up and pushed her strawberry blonde hair out of her face before struggling to her feet. Other than a few scrapes and a racing heartbeat, she wasn't hurt, thank the Goddess. Next to her, scaly rosettes of rhodiola crouched staunchly among the rocks. Amidst the dust, her minty-citrus scented insect repellant had become cloying. She pulled the crushed bottle from her bag and wrinkled her nose. Oily residue covered everything inside. She wiped her phone and the book on the leg of her jeans. At least she'd be insect-free for a while.

Along the cliff face behind her, a scoured swath of dirt and stone showed her path down the steep incline. It was a wonder she wasn't seriously injured. She peered both directions along the wall. Not one spot looked possible to climb.

"Fuck," she muttered. Her stutter never affected her curse words.

She turned back to the rhodiola. *Might as well make the most of the situation before I try to climb back up.* She pulled out her book to make sure the photos matched, then put on her gardening gloves and shoved a clump aside to get at the root. The plant seemed to grow directly from a crack in one of the large stones. If she could've used store-bought herbs, she would've, but for this potion, the rhodiola root had to be freshly gathered within seventy-two hours after a full moon.

Jabbing the pointed end of her trowel into the crack, she tried to pry it apart, but the tool scraped uselessly against the stone. She tried several angles, but the ground refused to give up its hold on the plant. Standing upright, she glared toward the overcast sky in frustration.

As if the heavens were laughing at her, a fat raindrop hit her square on the forehead. *Great.*

She wiped at the moisture with the back of one wrist, moving on to another nearby plant. All she succeeded in doing was breaking a fingernail down to the quick and snapping a few stems off at ground level. "I need these damn roots."

How could this be so hard? Her trowel didn't give her enough leverage against the rocks. She would have to come back with a full-sized shovel and try again. At least she knew where the rhodiola was now.

Stuffing her trowel and gloves back into her bag, she pulled out her phone to mark the spot on her app.

No reception.

She held the phone overhead and paced a few feet in either direction, waiting for a signal. The app refused to come up. Maybe the rock wall was blocking her. *God, what a day.*

Well, as long as she didn't stray from the wall, she wouldn't end up walking in circles. Eventually, she'd get reception again. Or at least find a relatively easy spot to climb and get back to the trail.

Phone in hand, she began walking along the base of the cliff.

CHAPTER THREE

Adrian stopped his ATV next to a blue Subaru Forester and cut the engine. What was a car doing so far off the road? He dismounted and circled the vehicle. Judging by the tire tracks, it'd only been here a few hours. A single set of footprints—a woman's, he'd guess by the size— headed straight toward a game trail that led to the moose kill site. He'd need to hurry if he wanted to catch her before she reached it.

He shouldered his rifle and started off, yearning for the ease of his mountain lion form. Where the trail veered to follow a ridge, a swath of fresh dirt marred the edge. Cautious of an undercut, he edged closer and peered over the drop-off. That landslide was definitely not the product of a controlled descent, but he didn't see a body. He called out, "Hello, anyone down there?"

Only wind rustling the leaves responded.

Sniffing the breeze, he tried to detect if the woman was still nearby. A delicious odor wafted toward him, masking all other scents and making his inner feline wriggle. *Catnip?* How strange.

Since the footprints ended here, he would have to investigate. He clambered down using his hands and feet. Descending as a mountain lion would've been easier, but approaching a frightened hiker as a predator was never a good idea, let alone one as rare as a mountain lion.

At the bottom, the strong essence of catnip made his feline instincts claw for attention. Reigning in his desire to shed his clothing and roll around on his back, he found the scuff marks of the woman's shoes and followed her trail.

Loose sand and random boulders made walking difficult, but the trail of catnip led him forward even when the footprints weren't clear. At a large tree, several limbs had been freshly broken, as if the woman had tried to climb up.

The scent of catnip was stronger here, as well as the delicious scent of female. Floral with a hint of sweet black tea, it reminded him of his early days with his mother, before his mountain lion had emerged, before the pack rejected him. A mountain lion didn't belong among wolves. He was what they called a "sport," an offspring with unexpected traits inherited from a long-ago ancestor.

The female scent in the area made his uniform trousers feel uncomfortably tight. *Mate*, his mountain lion purred. Adrian's balls agreed, but his head knew better. The catnip had to be messing with his senses. While he appreciated human females, he'd never met one who made him want to claim her. He was thinking about claiming this one sight-unseen.

And the heady scent was powerful, driving him forward even more than his duty to protect a hiker.

Ahead, another tree had four deep gouges staining the papery white trunk with lines of sap. *Claws.* This was a fresh bear marking. Adrian sniffed the air, senses muddied by warm female and dizzying catnip. The grizzly shifter had been here. Had made this mark. But something was off about the scent, a cloying, ashy odor that made bile rise in Adrian's throat. Randall's warning about an infection returned.

Running his tongue over his lengthening canines, Adrian

unslung his rifle and unlocked the safety. The female ahead was in danger. *My female,* his cat rumbled. Adrian couldn't deny the instinct. He picked up his pace to a run...

Get UNTAMED INSTINCT now!

ALSO BY TAMSIN LEY

Galactic Pirate Brides series

Galactic Pirate Brides Box Set (Includes first 3 books)

Rescued by Qaiyaan

Ransomed by Kashatok

Claimed by Noatak

Mates for Monsters

Mer-Lovers Collector's Edition (Includes first 3 books)

The Merman's Kiss

The Merman's Quest

A Mermaid's Heart

The Centaur's Bride

The Djinn's Desire

Khargals of Duras

Sticks and Stones

Alaska Alphas

Alpha Origins

Untamed Instinct

Bewitched Shifter

Midnight Heat

POST-APOCALYPTIC SCIENCE FICTION WRITTEN AS TAM LINSEY

Botanicaust

The Reaping Room

Doomseeds

Amarantox

ABOUT THE AUTHOR

Once upon a time I thought I wanted to be a biomedical engineer, but experimenting on lab rats doesn't always lead to happy endings. Now I blend my nerdy infatuation of science with character-driven romance and guaranteed happily-ever-afters. My monsters always find their mates, with feisty heroines, tortured heroes, and all the steamy trouble they can handle. I promise my stories will never leave you hanging (although you may still crave more!)

When I'm not writing, I'll be in the garden or the kitchen, exploring Alaska with my husband, or preparing for the zombie apocalypse. I also love wine and hard apple cider, am mediocre at crochet, and have the cutest 12-pound bunny named Abigail.

Interested in more about me? Join my VIP Club and get free books, notices, and other cool stuff!

www.tamsinley.com

bookbub.com/authors/tamsin-ley

goodreads.com/TamsinLey

facebook.com/TamsinLey

amazon.com/author/tamsin

CPSIA information can be obtained
at www.ICGtesting.com
Printed in the USA
LVHW081028060822
725338LV00015B/991